Midnight Auto Supply

Bob Puglisi

Cover design by Kym O'Connell-Todd

Bob Puglisi's photograph by Robert DeLaurenti

ISBN: 978-0-578-17644-4

Dedicated to all the guys from Corona, New York who lost their lives in the Vietnam War, and the ones wounded, physically and mentally, and to those who served.

U.S. involvement in the Vietnam War ended in 1972 with 58,169 American dead and 304,000 wounded. For the Vietnamese people, the war went on until 1975 when Saigon fell to the Communists.

Also By Bob Puglisi

Railway Avenue (A Novel)

Almost A Wiseguy with Vince Ciacci (A Memoir)
(Listen to more of Vince Ciacci's story at
www.mobshotpodcast.com)

Railway Avenue & Almost A Wiseguy
Are also available as e-books

CHAPTER 1

On a summer day in 1964, Frankie Russo prepares himself for one of the biggest days of his young life, but it turns out to be one of the worst, and it changes his life forever.

Frankie lives on a street with trees, modest one- and two-story houses. Mostly late model Chevys and Fords line both sides of the street. One of the cars, a 1954 two-tone, red and white Oldsmobile hardtop with chrome dual exhaust pipes extending from under the car and past the back bumper, belongs to Frankie's friend.

Frankie's brand-new 1964 Pontiac Bonneville, a white convertible with a black top and a black leather interior with bench seats, stands out among the rest of the cars. It has a back seat as wide as a small living room couch. Frankie's father doesn't drive because of failing eyesight so he buys Frankie a new car every year.

At about five-foot-four-inches tall, Frankie wears black chino pants and a white wife-beater T-shirt over his muscular chest. The twenty-one year old has brown hair and blue eyes. He holds a water hose and showers the Bonneville with water as his buddies busily soap the car.

Unlike his friends, Frankie has money in his pockets, expensive clothes, a good job with a steady income, a nice home, a girlfriend he loves, and not a care in the world. As a rich kid in a working-class community, some may consider Frankie an oddity.

At about the same age as Frankie, his best friend Benny Costanzo—everyone calls him Stanzo—has handsome looks, jet-black hair, and stands about five-feet-eight. Stanzo, a tough street kid, has proven himself many times in fights over the years.

Stanzo soaps the hood with a large sponge. He possesses the gift-of-gab and gets all the good-looking girls, something his friends envy. He wants to be a lawyer, an occupation in big demand in Corona, New York, where Frankie and his friends live.

Corona, a half-hour ride on the Flushing subway line to mid-town Manhattan, has a predominately Italian-American, blue-collar population.

Nicky Vittali, a twenty-year old, muscular, wiry-looking kid with little ambition, soaps the roof. He has blond hair and carries himself with the arrogance of someone you don't want to mess with. His friends call him crazy because they never know what he has up his sleeve. He likes to fight and get drunk. But Nicky also has artistic abilities, and designs and draws tattoos for his friends.

Frankie's other friend, twenty-two year old Charlie Ferraro, a tall skinny guy, with brown hair and a mischievous looking smile, stands on the sidewalk watching his friends wash the car. Charlie, a graduate of Aviation High School, a vocational school for the aviation industry, wants be an aircraft mechanic, but cleans planes for a small cargo airline at La Guardia

Airport. You have to watch Charlie around your girlfriend. Charlie always tries to make it with somebody's girl. Charlie owns the Oldsmobile. He loves fast cars and girls.

Ricky Cruz, a big, tall, twenty-year old with black curly hair, wears glasses with black frames. He has been in the states since the Cuban revolution. Ricky, a recent college dropout, works at the A&P Supermarket to save enough money to buy his first car.

Ricky flings his soapy sponge at Nicky but misses and hits Charlie in the back of the head. Charlie grabs the hose away from Frankie and tries to spray Ricky, but hits Stanzo and the water sprays Nicky as well. Stanzo retaliates by emptying a bucket of soapy water on Charlie. The whole scene turns into a wild melee as they run around throwing water at each other.

A half hour later, the Bonneville looks dry and sparkling, but not Frankie and his friends who are soaking wet. As they stand in front of the car, Frankie pops the hood and they all stare at the large engine. Frankie with a dry rag in his hand shines the large, round chrome air filter crowning the four-banger carburetor. The guys stare at the impressive engine with admiration. "It's 421 cubic inches and 320 horsepower," Frankie boasts.

"We ought to take it out to the drag strip in West Hampton," Nicky says.

"That's all I gotta do. My old man will kill me. He's already warned me about having accidents."

"How many you had so far—five?" Charlie laughs.

"Don't make it worse than it is. It's only three."

"So far," Charlie replies sarcastically.

Frankie reaches up, pulls down the hood and slams it shut.

Stanzo looks at Frankie and asks, "Ya ain't gonna go through with this are you?"

Frankie nods and his friends register their disapproval.

"Don't do it man," Charlie warns.

Frankie picks up sponges and the bucket. Stanzo grabs the hose as they head towards the house. "Hey man, I'll fix you up with some good-lookin' chicks."

"I'm not like you. I want to settle down, have a family. Besides I'm gonna get drafted if I don't get married. They're not drafting married guys."

Out in the street Charlie's car starts with a blast of exhaust and loud rock and roll music. The Four Seasons' "Dawn" blares out of the radio. The horn blows for Stanzo. From the edge of the alley, Stanzo waves. "I'm coming."

"I'd probably do it too if I met the right one," Stanzo says.

Charlie holds the horn down. "Awright, good luck with Gloria. Maybe we'll see ya at Al's tonight."

"Yeah, thanks."

Stanzo turns, walks to Charlie's car and gets in the front seat next to Ricky. Nicky, still horsing around behind the car, looks over to see the Oldsmobile quickly accelerate away from the curb, leaving Nicky standing there. Frankie stands in front of his house and watches with amusement as Nicky chases after the Olds. The car slows down for him and just as he catches up with it, Charlie accelerates again, then stops. This time Nicky runs and manages to grab the frame of the back window and pulls himself through the open window. After a burst of speed, screeching tires, and loud exhaust the car cruises down the block.

CHAPTER 2

Frankie comes out of the standup glass shower with a towel around his waist. He grabs a dry hand towel from the rack and wipes the moisture off the medicine cabinet mirror over the bathroom sink. From the cabinet he grabs a razor and shaving cream, and then soaps his face. With several quick strokes of the razor, Frankie has a clean-shaven face. He wipes away the excess shaving cream with the hand towel. He opens the cabinet again, reaches for a large bottle of English Leather, and splashes it on his chest, neck, and face. His hand still wet with cologne, looks at himself in the mirror, and down at the towel around his waist, puts his hand inside, and brushes his genitals with cologne.

"Whew," he bristles from the sting.

Frankie grabs a tube of Brylcreem, squeezes a small amount of the white cream and slathers it through his hair. He combs his hair back, and with his free hand pulls some curly hair forward over his forehead. He picks up underarm deodorant and wipes it under one arm, then the other. After one final check in the mirror he tosses the towel aside, leaves the bathroom and steps into his bedroom.

Frankie has a spacious bedroom, with expensive mahogany furniture, a double size bed with head and footboard, and two small night tables with lamps. The wall in front of the bed has a waist-high dresser, and a rectangular mirror with a mahogany frame that hangs on the wall. Frankie opens the top drawer and grabs a white t-shirt, shorts, and a pair of black socks. He tosses the socks on his bed and slips on the t-shirt and shorts.

He enters his walk-in closet with its expensive neatly hung clothing. Frankie passes up a black shirt and opts for a stiff white one with long pointed spread collars that he puts on and buttons. He removes the pants of a gray sharkskin suit from the hanger and slips them on. From a hanging tie rack, he selects a narrow black tie and tosses it around his neck. He comes out of the closet carrying his suit jacket and carefully places it over the footboard of his bed.

Frankie sits on the edge of the bed and puts on socks. From under his bed, he pulls expensive-looking Florsheim black penny loafers. He picks up a shoe brush and gives them a quick swipe, then slips them on. Frankie stands and walks over to his dresser, opens a jewelry box and grabs several pieces of expensive jewelry, rings, a watch, and a gold ID bracelet. He flips his tie into a knot, buttons the top button, tightens, and straightens his tie into place.

Frankie puts on his suit jacket and checks his appearance in the mirror. From the dresser, he picks up a black ring box and shoves it into his inside breast pocket. He looks at a high school graduation picture of his girlfriend, Gloria on one end of his dresser, then over at the other end of the dresser he looks at a picture of his mother in her wedding gown. He smiles at the picture, kisses his index and middle finger, and presses them to the picture. "Wish me luck, Ma."

As Frankie walks down the hallway to the living room, the voice of a TV news journalist says, "...Eight U.S. servicemen were wounded in Vietnam when a terrorist bomb was thrown into a crowd. The Servicemen were standing on a dock viewing the sunken USS *Card*, an escort carrier sunk by a terrorist bomb the day before. Vietcong terrorists are suspected of both explosions..."

Albert Russo, sixtyish, slightly balding with thick glasses, and overweight sits in an easy chair. The comfortable-looking room has expensive, overstuffed chairs and furnishings. Family pictures hang on the wall behind Albert. He looks away from the television when Frankie enters. "Hey, you're looking pretty sharp."

"Thanks, Pop."

Fourteen-year-old Frankie had lost his mom to cancer, and Frankie took it hard. So did Albert, and Frankie's older brother Anthony, and sister Mary, who both live in New Jersey with their families. Frankie and his father look out for one another. Albert and his younger brother Ralph own an Italian restaurant, Russo's, in Manhattan's theater district, where Frankie works as the manager several nights a week.

"This Vietnam thing is getting worse. I saw Tommy Martino's mother at church this morning. She says Tommy got his token" (A practice at the time of sending a New York City subway token with the draft notice).

"Yeah?"

"I'm worried about you havin' to go over there."

"Don't worry Pop. I'm gettin' married. They ain't drafting married guys."

Worry creases Albert's face nevertheless. "Not now they're not." The two stare blankly at each other for a moment. "So ya got the ring?"

Frankie reaches inside his suit and pulls out the ring box. "Yeah."

"Uncle Vito give ya a good deal?" Albert's older brother, Vito, owns a jewelry store on Manhattan's Lower Eastside.

"Yeah... have a look," as he opens the box and holds it out for his father.

His dad's smile broadens as he takes in the impressive diamond engagement ring. "Oh, yeah— that's a nice one. Half a carat?"

"Nah, one carat. He gave it to me for the same price as half."

"I'll send him over a case of wine. Ya know how he loves a nice Chianti."

"That'll be nice. I gotta run, Pop. I'm gonna pick up Gloria and drive into the city for dinner at Tavern on the Green. That's where I'll ask her and give her the ring."

With a gleam in his eyes, Albert says, "Ah that sounds very romantic."

"Ya need any smokes, Pop?" Albert feels the pack of Lucky Strikes lying on the couch arm.

"Nah, I got enough. Ya got money?"

Albert reaches into his pants pocket, removes a wad of cash in a silver money clip, and places it next to the cigarettes. Frankie looks down at the money and considers the offer.

"Awright. Good luck. Watch your driving. Remember what I told ya."

"Yeah."

His father means accidents. Frankie claims the accidents hadn't been his fault.

Frankie starts to leave, then turns back, looks at the money again. This time he reaches down and removes the cash from the clip, leaving just the clip, and pockets the dough. "Thanks Pop." Frankie turns and leaves.

Albert looks over his shoulder, shakes his head with a playful smile, and turns his attention back to the television.

CHAPTER 3

Frankie comes out the front door of his house, a bright flash of lightening and loud clap of thunder greets him. A downpour quickly ensues. Frankie registers his annoyance with a smirk as he looks up at the sky. He pulls the collar of his suit jacket up around his neck, grabs his lapels, and holds them tight as he swaggers down the front steps over to his shiny and now wet car. He unlocks the door and gets in.

Frankie settles into the seat and inserts the key into the ignition. He turns the key and the powerful engine turns over easily. The Beatles "She Loves Me," blares from the radio, drowning out the rumble of the engine. Frankie relaxes into the plush black leather bench seat as he shifts the car into drive and steps on the gas.

The rear wheels of the Bonneville spin and screech on the wet pavement as the car rapidly pulls out of the parking spot. It fishtails slightly then heads down the street and turns left at the corner.

Frankie drives by Linden Park, where he and his friends had hung out. He glances at the wet empty park and removes a Marlboro from a box, lights it with the car lighter. As he inhales, he reminisces about hanging out in the park and the fights they had there with black and Puerto Rican gangs from the other side of 37th Avenue.

The Bonneville accelerates and turns up another street heading away from the park. Rain falls heavily as the car approaches the next intersection. The traffic light turns red. Frankie slows the Bonneville as he approaches the empty intersection. Before the light turns green again, Frankie glances in both directions, but instead of stopping completely for the light he accelerates through it.

Frankie has made this a habit. He doesn't worry about traffic tickets because he knows most of the cops in the neighborhood. In fact, he knows policemen all over the city and can usually talk his way out of a ticket by dropping a name or two. On occasion, he has given officers his restaurant's business card with a promise of a free drink, dinner, or both.

At the next few red lights, Frankie slows down then accelerates through the intersection. The rain changes to a light drizzle on the empty streets. The Bonneville's right turn signal flashes as Frankie approaches a corner a little too fast.

A football flies through the air; two young boys follow its flight. As soon as he turns the corner, Frankie notices the boys coming towards him. He quickly cranks the wheel to avoid hitting them.

The kids jump out of the way just as the Pontiac skids past them. The Bonneville heads towards a car at the curb. Frankie cranks the wheel violently in the other direction. The big car veers away from that car and its rear end narrowly misses another car. The football players scatter. The Bonneville slides across the narrow one-way street. It jumps the curb and comes to an abrupt stop as the right front side crashes into a fire hydrant, sending high-pressure water shooting into the air, like a gushing oil well.

A shaken Frankie catches his breath, crushes out his cigarette, turns the car off, and gets out. The boys stand aghast and visibly shaken; they keep backing out of range of the water. A few people come out of their houses; others stick their heads out windows. A neighbor yells from an upstairs window, "Hey! Everybody awright?"

Frankie looks at the boys. "Everyone okay?"

The boys nod. "Everybody's okay," Frankie tells the man at the window.

Frankie walks around the back of the car trying to avoid the hydrant water, coming down worse than the rain. He looks from a distance at the damage he has done to the front end of his car and at the broken fire hydrant lying on the ground.

Frankie, noticeably upset, slams his fist on the trunk, and then gets back into the car. He thinks to himself, *fuck, fuck, fuck, my new car. I had another accident.* He starts the car, turns on the windshield wipers, and shifts into reverse. The rear wheels screech but the car barely moves. Frankie puts the car back into park. He leaves the car running, removes the key from the ignition, and gets out of the car.

Frankie unlocks the trunk and removes a jack handle. He tries to go to the front of the car to use the jack handle to try prying the fender away from the wheel. He has to make a hasty retreat as water drenches him. The kids find it comical watching Frankie in his best clothes getting wet. He attempts a weak smile in their direction and quickly runs out of range of the water.

A police car turns the corner and comes to a stop near Frankie's car. Frankie looks at them and forces a smile as the two police officers get out of the car and survey the scene. One of them, an overweight guy with a big belly, says, "From those skid marks, you're lucky it wasn't worse."

"Tell me about it." Frankie looks at the boys who have come closer to the car and nervously toss the football between them.

The police officer takes out a traffic ticket book. "Let me see your license and registration."

Frankie says, "Ya know Captain Kelly?"

"Captain Kelly? Yeah, we're in his division."

"He's a good friend of mine."

"Oh yeah? How'd ya know Kelly?"

"He comes to our restaurant in the city; Russo's on 45th Street…"

"Yeah? Kelly likes to eat."

The other cop, a tall guy about the same age as the other one, says, "He likes his scotch, too."

"Oh, yeah," Frankie says. The two police officers smile understandingly at each other.

"Tell him Frankie Russo says, 'hi!'"

The tall cop says, "I better go call the water guys to turn this damn thing off."

The overweight cop puts his ticket book back in his pocket. "We better wait for them before we try to move your car."

Hours later, Frankie sits on Gloria's couch; his hair and clothing still wet from the rain. With all his plans in the toilet, he feels anxious. His girlfriend, Gloria Rizzo sits next to him.

Gloria lives in a two-story house on the borderline of Corona and Elmhurst. Her living room has modern-looking, expensive furniture. Her father, Joe, a life insurance sales representative for the Metropolitan Life Insurance Company, got his daughter a job in the typing pool at his company's headquarters in Manhattan, following her graduation from Flushing High School. Gloria's mom, Louise, a housewife, only had one job before her marriage to Joe.

Twenty-year old, Gloria, a cute, petite blonde with a shapely body and blue eyes, met Frankie at a party about a year ago. Gloria, an only child, gets whatever she wants from her parents. She loves clothes and has quite a wardrobe. Tonight, unlike her usual stylish dress, Gloria wears a robe and has big rollers in her hair.

"...You show up two hours late. You had an accident... you have no car... and it's raining."

"Ay, I can't help the weather."

"Well ya didn't have to have an accident."

"Don't remind me. I didn't want to have an accident. I still have to tell my old man. And I'm gonna have to pay for a new fire hydrant..." Frankie turns on his most romantic smile and says, "I'm sorry everything went all wrong. I didn't plan it this way."

"Well what are we gonna do now?"

"We can still go to the city. We'll just take a cab."

"Ooo, cabs are so dirty."

"You wanna take the train then?"

Gloria scrunches up her face. "No! I hate that train. I have to ride it all week to work."

"Well, then, let's go somewhere around here."

"How we gonna get there? It's raining."

"Ya ever hear of walkin'?" He says, a little too angry.

"Don't get smart. I hate walking in the rain."

With a twinkle in his eyes, Frankie says, "Why? It's romantic."

Gloria sulks and folds her arms across her chest.

Disappointment registers on Frankie's face. He stares at Gloria—wanting to say something comforting, but words won't come. Finally, out of desperation, he reaches into his jacket and removes the ring box. "I wanted this to be special, but here goes."

Frankie opens the box, revealing the diamond ring. Gloria gazes into the distance. Frankie kneels on one knee at her feet and takes her hand. Gloria's eyes widen incredulously as she notices the diamond for the first time. She looks back and forth between the ring and Frankie.

"Gloria will you take this ring and marry me?"

Gloria's mouth drops open. "Frankie..."

With pride and love written all over his face, Frankie carefully removes the ring from the box and places it on her finger. Frankie half stands and kisses her gently on the lips. Gloria remains frozen. Sensing something wrong, he removes his lips, steps back and stares at her. "Ain't ya gonna say somethin'?"

"I don't know what to say."

"Ya can start with I will."

"I don't know if I want to."

"Whatta ya mean? We've been talkin' about this."

"I mean I don't know if I'm ready. I... I..."

"I love ya. You love me. I wanna marry ya."

"Well... Well..."

"What?" All the color drains from Frankie's face, crushing the moment for him.

"I have to think about it."

"Think about it! Think about it! What's to think about?"

Gloria stares at the ring. Frankie sighs. Her blue eyes look up at him. His shoulders slump and he heads for the door. Disappointment lines his face. Frankie opens the door and leaves. *How can this day get any worse*?

"Frankie! Frankie!" Gloria shouts after him.

CHAPTER 4

Light drizzle falls on the busy intersection of Roosevelt Avenue and 108th Street. In this part of Queens, the Flushing subway line sits above Roosevelt Avenue and casts dark shadowy images on the street below. The trains on this line carry passengers to and from Manhattan and Flushing.

Frankie looks like a fish out of water as he walks to the corner across from Al's Bar and Grill. He thinks to himself, *I can't believe Gloria's reaction. What am I gonna tell the guys?* All the while, the rock and roll ballad, "If You Lose Me," by Barbara Lynn, replays in his head.

Al's Bar & Grill a typical old neighborhood watering hole, dimly lit, and barely a step up from seedy has been second home for Frankie and his friends. The walls and floor give off the aroma of years of tap beer that assaults the nostrils even before you enter. The main bar area has several red leather booths with tables against the window; the back room has a pool table and wooden phone booth. A dartboard hangs on the wall next to the bar. Neon beer signs for Ballantine, Rheingold, and Schaefer hang in the windows and around the bar area. They throw off deep blue, green, and hot pink light. Soffits around the walls provide the rest of the light inside the bar.

Charlie and Ricky wear black clothes, and toss darts at the board. In the background, a TV newscaster drones on with the latest news. "…The Ford Motor Company announced today that it has retooled for its 1965 Mustang with a new 200 horsepower, 289 cubic inch engine as its base V8…" "I'm getting me one of those," Charlie says.

"Looks like a cool car," Ricky says.

Al Cappa stands behind the bar drying glasses with a towel and watching television. Al owns the place, but the liquor license has someone else's name on it because of Al's police record. He got that during his days as a member of the Corona Outlaws, a street gang with a citywide reputation as one of the toughest in the city during the 1950s. Al had several arrests for his involvement in gang fights. At nineteen, they sent him to an upstate correctional facility for three years after holding up a liquor store with a gun.

Al is thirtyish, stands about six feet tall, with a medium build, and handsome face. Frankie and his friends consider Al a cool guy. They love to listen to his stories about, as they call it, "the old days in Corona." Al is the only older person that they think has any good advice. He looks like the kind of guy you'd want on your side in a fight.

Frankie and his friends have been hanging out at Al's since before they reached the drinking age of eighteen. Al has never asked any of them for proof of age.

The TV news journalist says, "...Vietcong terrorists are suspected of both explosions." Al snaps off the television. "This goddamn war... If we fought our battles around here like these assholes in Washington— who knows what this neighborhood would be like?"

Charlie and Nicky toss their last darts and sit at the bar. Nicky says, "They don't know what the hell they're doin'. My old man was in the South Pacific on some Jap held island when they dropped the first one. He says they knew the war was gonna be over soon."

"That Truman was a son-of-a-bitch. He fried the Japs' asses," Al says.

Stanzo says, "It ain't gonna last long. My old man was in D-day." He says, "'They hit the Nazis with everything they had before the invasion.' All we gotta do is bomb the shit outta them like we did the Nazi's. Wipe the sonsa-bitches off the face of the earth."

"Yeah smart ass, so why ain't we? I gotta bad feeling about this one. We never fought a war like this before."

"Whatta ya mean?" Stanzo asks.

"It's guerrilla warfare. They run around in pajamas and sandals, and they hit ya and run," Al says.

"You're so worried, call the White House," Stanzo says.

Al notices Nicky busily doodling on the bar with a pencil. "How many times I gotta tell ya? Not on my bar!"

The two exchange unfriendly glances as Al wipes away Nicky's handiwork with a wet rag. Al hands Nicky a bunch of napkins. "Here! Use these."

Al stands in front of Nicky to make sure he draws on the napkins. "You assholes better start worrying about the draft," waving a finger at all of them.

"Shit—I'm goin' back to school before they draft me," Ricky boasts.

"That's if they don't getcha first," Al tells him.

"They draft me; I go back to Cooba."

Charlie adds his two-cents. "Yeah, you go back to Cooba. Castro'll grab your ass so fast... You'll either wind up in jail or in the Cooban Army."

They all laugh at Ricky's expense.

Al says, "You go back, you're a political prisoner. Ya know that?"

"Boolshit—my family don't do nothin' political. My old man wassa waiter."

Al laughs. "Waiter! Waiters are the first to get locked up."

"Boolshit!"

"They don't fuckin' care." Snapping his fingers, "They'll lock you up so fast—and throw away the key."

"Boolshit, Al. Joo go in the Army. They cut all joor hair off."

"Man! That's what you're worried about?"

"Not only that... I'm not leavin' Corona." Then he mumbles something quickly in Spanish.

Nicky pipes in, "Yeah—they want me to kill gooks—they gotta bring 'em here."

An astonished Al says, "Would you listen to this... Yeah, we'll just go over there and say, 'hey fellas, we wanna have a war with ya—but one thing—ya gotta come to Corona, fuckin' Queens to fight."

Stanzo says, "Well they ain't gonna draft me."

"Oh, why? You're so special?" Al asks.

"I'm 4-F. I only got one kidney."

"Bullshit," Al says.

Nicky says, "It's true. The asshole's only got one kidney.

Ricky asks, "Yeah, only one kidney?" Stanzo nods that it's true.

"No shit! Well, there's your answer. Have a kidney cut out,"Al says."

"Shit, I'll cut mine out if it keeps me out of the army," Nicky pipes in.

Charlie asks, "What about you, Al?"

"They won't take me. I got a record. Beside who's gonna run this joint? You assholes?"

Stanzo says, "Joey the Duck got his notice this week."

"Joey the Duck? You're kidding. When's he goin'," Nicky asks.

"Two weeks."

"Joey the Duck!" Charlie laughs. "They take him— you know they're desperate. Better watch out guys!" He warns. "Imagine the Duck marching with the troops." They all burst out laughing.

The laughter stops when they notice Frankie coming through the front door with wet clothes and water dripping from his hair. They watch him swagger up to the bar and throw a hundred-dollar bill down. "Al, give me a seven and seven! And give everybody a round. You too, Al."

Al asks, "You hoofin' it?"

"Yeah. Had an accident this afternoon."

"With the new car?" Stanzo asks.

"Yeah."

Frankie removes his wet suit jacket and places it on the back of his bar stool. "Ya got a towel, Al?"

Al puts down the bottle he's pouring from, reaches under the bar, and throws Frankie a dry towel. "So what's this—number two? Al asks.

"Number four."

"I thought ya were givin' Gloria the ring?" Stanzo asks.

As Frankie wipes his wet hair with the towel, he answers, "I did. I had the accident so she got pissed that I was late, and didn't have the car. Now she doesn't know if she wants to marry me." All the while, that damn song "If You Lose Me," keeps playing in Frankie's head.

"Didn't your old man tell ya he's not paying for any more accidents?" Stanzo asks.

Frankie nods a reluctant yes. It reminds him of what his father told him. *Watch your driving.* Al places a coaster and drink in front of Frankie, then pours the others. The guys raise their glasses in a gesture of appreciation. Al raises his glass as well and, mimics Gloria, "I can't marry ya Frankie baby, if ya don't have your wheels."

They all laugh; some mimic Gloria as well until Stanzo says, "Hey, leave 'im alone."

"I told ya this one's just goin' out with ya for your money," Al says. Al playfully slaps Frankie's cheek with a weak jab. Frankie puts up his fists and the two spar over the bar, but Frankie proves no match for Al's quick hands. "Wake up—*stunad.*" The other's laugh. "This broad's the reason you're havin' accidents. What are ya laughin' at?" He asks the guys. "The only thing that makes you assholes different than him—he's got money. The rest of ya don't have a pot to piss in."

Stanzo asks Frankie, "Whatta ya gonna tell your old man?"

"I don't know. I don't know how I'm gonna pay for it."

With the wave of his hand, Al says, "Ah, ya can afford it."

"Nah, I'm broke. I blew a shitload on the ring and a bundle last night. The old man gave me another 200 bucks this afternoon. And I'm gonna have to pay for a new fire hydrant."

"Ya hit a hydrant? Stanzo asks. His friends all laugh.

"Yeah, it could have been worse. I just missed some kids. Then, Gloria gives me this… 'I don't know if I'm ready to get married.' Geez, ya know how many times we talked about it? I thought she wanted to get married."

"See that's the difference between you and me. I get whatever I want from these broads and don't even buy 'em a drink," Stanzo says.

"Yeah, well joo're a cheap bastard," Ricky says.

"Fuck you!"

"When was the last time joo buy us a drink?

"I'm always buyin'."

They all laugh. Stanzo throws a twenty-dollar bill on the bar. "Al, the next round's on me."

Applause and cheers follow. Stanzo frowns and gives them the finger. "Hey, I gotta call Linda." Stanzo gets up and walks to the telephone booth in the back.

"Al, if he's buyin', give me a Cuba Libre." Ricky smiles mischievously.

Al looks at Frankie and says, "I always say, if the broad's worth it, ya spend a few bucks on her. It doesn't hurt. That's somethin' ya gotta learn. That's why me and Anita have been together so long. Ya gotta know the one's ya spend your dough on. But this one... Did ya at least get laid last night?"

A shitty grin crosses Frankie's face. Stanzo pats Frankie on the back. "See, that's alright then," Al says. His friends laugh.

Stanzo sits in the phone booth. He listens to the phone ring waiting for Linda Pinnella his girlfriend of six months to answer. It has been a rocky relationship.

A sweet voice at the other end says, "Hello."

"Hi, it's me."

"I thought it was you."

"How'd ya know that?"

"I just knew."

"You're too smart."

"Yeah, right."

"Whatta ya doin'?"

"Studying."

"Man, ya study too much. Can ya go out tonight?" Stanzo twists the phone cord around his finger.

"Maybe later when I finish studying."

"Man, you're always studyin'."

"Yeah, well if you did, you'd still be in college." Stanzo knows he has heard this from her before.

"Don't worry about me. I'm goin' back as soon as I save enough for a car."

"I'm glad to hear that. You're too smart to be wasting your life away in a mailroom, Benny."

"Thanks for the vote of confidence. So ya gonna come out?"

"Come over around nine."

"Awright, I'll see ya later." Stanzo hangs up and leaves the phone booth.

Stanzo returns to the bar and sits next to Frankie. "So whatta ya gonna do about the car?" Stanzo asks.

"I'll take it to Lorenzo's to get an estimate tomorrow. I figure, maybe five, six-hundred."

"That's tough," Charlie says.

"Save your money. There's always midnight auto supply. We used to do it all the time. Ya just go out and find another Pontiac like yours and steal it for the parts." Al gazes around the bar and lowers his voice. "Did I ever tell ya about the time I blew the engine on my '53 Merc drag racing? We went out, found another '53 Merc, and swapped engines. We even stole a tow truck and towed the car back, all in one night."

"Bullshit," Stanzo says.

"Hey Stanzo, that's no shit."

"Sure—just like that. Come on Al!" Charlie says. Al waves his hand at him.

Al says to Frankie, "You can have your wheels fixed before your old man finds out."

"Where we gonna find another white Pontiac, Bonneville convertible?" Stanzo asks.

"First of all... Ya don't have to find a convertible. Just a white '64 Bonneville. They're around. I see them all the time."

Nicky adds, "Yeah man, they're around. I see 'em too. Let's do it."

"You're nuts. How's he gonna find another car like his and get it fixed by tomorrow?" Stanzo argues.

Al preaches: "Get off your asses and go look for one. Whatta ya gonna do, sit around here all night talkin' about it?"

"Shit—if we can find a car like yours, we can fix it by tomorrow," Nicky says confidently.

Frankie seems to be mulling over his options. He laments, "That's all I gotta do is get caught stealin' a car."

"Only idiots who do stupid things get caught," Al says, pointing his finger for emphasis.

"Joo get caught—it can keep joo from gettin' drafted," Ricky adds.

"Marrying Gloria will keep me out of the army."

Nicky laughs, "Steal the car, man. Come on, let's just see if we can find a car like yours."

Frankie sips his drink. "I don't know. What about Danny Boy DeSantis?"

"DeSantis is an asshole. And he got a suspended sentence. And he don't have to worry about gettin' drafted, either." Nicky says.

"Yeah, it was easy. They had pass keys to a lot of different cars," Charlie says.

"Not getting drafted. That's not so bad. Shit, if I don't get married soon, they're gonna call me any day," Frankie says.

"So, let's go. We can do this," Nicky says.

"You're fuckin' crazy. Steal a car?" Stanzo points to Al and says, "Don't listen to this crazy bastard."

"What if we get caught?" Frankie asks.

"Only idiots who do stupid things after they steal it get caught." Al says.

"First off, how do ya know you're gonna find a car?" Stanzo says.

Frankie knows it may not be that easy, takes a sip of his drink, and says, "Al's right. We don't have to find a convertible. Just any white '64... I guess we can take a look. It's worth a shot."

Al smiles and Nicky says, "We can do this."

Charlie says, "Yeah!" How ya gonna find this car? Take the bus?" Everyone laughs.

Frankie looks at Charlie. "Only thing—we need a car to get there... Charlie?"

Charlie hopelessly looks around the bar avoiding the obvious. Finally, he says, "I ain't stealin' a car."

"Me neither," Stanzo says.

"So lend him your car," Al says.

"I ain't lendin' him my car."

"You jerks want to go to jail—count me out," Stanzo says.

Al says, "Friends like you—ya don't need enemies."

"That's a cliché," Stanzo answers.

"Cliché bullshit," Al says.

Al turns away and walks to the other end of the bar to take care of a new customer.

"Come on Cha—lee. Don't be a prick. Give us joo car."

Charlie gives him the finger. "No. I got things to do."

Al, hearing this, walks back over. "What?"

"Things. I don't have to tell you assholes everything I do."

Al says, "You're gonna sit here like you do every night nursin' a beer and tryin' to pick up somebody else's broad." The guys laugh, knowingly.

"You lend him your car."

"Nobody drives my car but me."

A little frustrated, Charlie replies, "Oh see... Yeah, well nobody drives my car but me."

"Boolshit! We always drive joo car," Ricky reminds him.

Frankie says, "Leave him alone." He turns to Charlie and says, "It's okay."

"If ya wanna wait till two when I close this joint I'll take ya."

"Nah, that's okay Al. We probably ain't gonna be able to find another car like mine anyway."

Ricky looks at Charlie with contempt. "Prick!"

Charlie returns Ricky's gaze with his middle finger.

Nicky stands next to Charlie and pleads, "We'll just go out and look and we'll bring it right back."

"Hey, quit breakin' his balls. Don't let them suck ya in Charlie. This is a stupid idea," Stanzo says.

"Come on, Charl? We'll just go out and look for a while and we'll bring it right back." Nicky says.

"I gotta be home by nine."

An excited Nicky replies, "We'll be back by nine."

"Ya betta. Frankie drives! I don't want you assholes drivin' my car." They look at him with hurt expressions and surprise as Charlie tosses Frankie the keys.

Stanzo shakes his head in disapproval, then at Charlie and says, "Big mistake, asshole."

They all jump off their stools, down drinks, pick up money from the bar, and grab their jackets. Frankie turns to Stanzo and asks, "Ya comin'?"

"Nah, I got a date with Linda."

Al gives them the thumbs up. Stanzo watches them head for the door, and shouts, "Hey wait up!"

They stop and turn around. Frankie says, "I thought you got a date?"

"I'm not lettin' ya go by yourselves. Just drop me off at Linda's by nine."

Charlie reminds them, "Nine o'clock. Don't forget!"

The guys come out of the bar, turn right and walk down the street. Nicky says, "Hey look, it stopped raining."

But the streets still look wet and a chilling dampness remains in the air.

"...Ya think you're gonna find another car like yours and get it fixed by tomorrow?" Stanzo asks Frankie.

Ricky answers, "They're 'round, man. Joo see them all the time."

"Yeah man, I see 'em too. If we can find one, we can fix it by tomorrow," Nicky boasts.

"Bullshit!" Stanzo adds.

They find Charlie's car. Frankie gets in on the driver's side. Nicky and Ricky climb in the back while Stanzo sits in the passenger seat next to Frankie as the car pulls away. "I don't know why you listen to that crazy bastard Al," Stanzo says to Frankie.

Hanging over the front seat, "Hey man, we can do it," Nicky reminds them.

Stanzo turns around to Nicky, "First of all, if you even find one, how ya gonna get in, and then how ya gonna get it started?"

"Ya get in with a coat hanger."

"Ya got a coat hanger? Stanzo asks. Nicky screws up his face. "Yeah, see what I mean. Three hours to get in Charlie's car when he locked his keys inside. And that was two o'clock on a Sunday afternoon and we weren't worried about getting caught."

"'Cause this is a hardtop. Convertibles are easy to get in," Ricky says.

"Yeah," Nicky adds.

"Oh yeah… you know? How many convertibles did you break into?" Stanzo asks.

"My old man had a convertible once. We got in quick with the hanger," Ricky says.

"You got in? You got in?"

"Well I was there." Stanzo proves his point; he turns around and rests his case.

"I can get in. And hot wiring it's so easy I can do it with my eyes closed," Nicky says.

"Yeah, how many cars have ya hot-wired?" Stanzo asks.

"Awright quit arguing," Frankie scolds.

The Oldsmobile cruises slowly down one street after another as the guys look out the windows on both sides of the car.

"Man, I haven't seen one Pontiac," Ricky says out of frustration.

"Isn't it the way when you're looking for something you don't find it," Frankie says.

"This is stupid. We're gonna be out here all night. Why don't ya just tell your old man?" Stanzo asks.

"I'll have to."

"Your not gonna find a car like that," Stanzo tells him.

"Yeah, you're probably right."

The car moves a lot faster as it whizzes by all makes and models. They drive through commercial districts with different size stores and shops selling all types of merchandise. They go up and down streets with a mix of small and large apartment buildings; one-, two-, and three-family houses. They pass all types of cars but not one white '64.

"You're not gonna find a car like yours around here. We're looking in the wrong neighborhoods. We should go to Flushing or Bayside—Forest Hills," Stanzo says. Finally, the Oldsmobile stops in front of Linda's house. Linda lives in a single-family house in Corona Heights. She has a big family, most of which live on the same street.

"Be careful. I'll see ya later." Stanzo jumps out of the car and Nicky climbs into the front seat.

As they pull away, "Man he's a pain in the ass," Ricky says.

He's probably right, Frankie thinks to himself. *He usually is. I'm just gonna have to face my old man. I should probably call Gloria when I get back to Al's. I should have stayed at Al's in the first place.*

CHAPTER 5

Al's Bar & Grill looks busier now as it usually does later in the evening when the regulars arrive and sit in their favorite spots.

Buck, an old barfly and former dockworker in his sixties, sits at the end of the bar. He has a half empty glass of beer in front of him. Buck wears an old black wool cap over his mostly bald head. He wears that hat year round. Nicky took it off his head once and almost had his arm broken by Buck. As the evening goes on, Buck's head sinks closer to the bar, and by the end of the night, it sits atop the bar with him out cold. He leaves it up to Al to wake him, get him on his feet, and drive him home.

Three neighborhood girls, Angela Scotti, Pinky DeAngelo, and Maryanne Marconi, sit at the bar next to Charlie who nervously watches the clock, now approaching nine. Angela and Pinkie look like tough girls.

Angela, barely five feet tall, wears her brown hair in a ponytail. She dresses predominately in black with a black leather jacket over a tight black sweater and tight black pants. She looks pretty with round cheeks, blue eyes, and a stocky body. In high school, and despite her small stature, she became the star of her basketball and volleyball teams. She likes Nicky, and the two have gone out occasionally.

Pinky and Angela have been best friends since kindergarten. Pinky towers over Angela, and together they have a Mutt and Jeff appearance. Pinky has blond hair and big boobs for a skinny girl; the guys love those breasts. Charlie took Pinkie to her high school prom, and on dates for a few months. The other guys envy Charlie for that honor. Pinky, a beauty culture student, always dresses nice, and her nails and hair always look good. Tonight, she wears a red v-neck sweater over tight white pants.

On the other hand, Maryanne, a little too sweet and gentle for this crowd is barely five feet tall, cute, with a petite body, shoulder-length curly brown hair and an olive complexion. She's been hanging around with this group since junior high, just after moving from Brooklyn. Maryanne attends St. John's University on a full scholarship, majoring in education. She and Frankie had been an item for a short time until Frankie met Gloria. Stanzo claims she has no tits, and it keeps him from going out with her.

"So ya still goin' to school for that hair stuff," Charlie asks Pinkie.

"Yeah, of course! Hair, nails, and makeup. I'm gonna go to work in my uncle's funeral parlor when I graduate."

"I wouldn't go telling too many people if I were you."

"Why? It's a good business, Charlie. People like their relatives to look good when they kick the bucket."

Charlie laughs. "Yeah, they're dying to get in."

Pinkie punches him hard in the bicep. "Ow!" Charlie howls.

"You're a real scream, Charlie."

Eddie and Hanna Callahan, a couple in their fifties who like their booze, sit a few seats down from Charlie. Eddie, overweight with red hair, collects trash for the city. Hanna, a short, thin, wisp of a woman with curly red hair works for the post office. With the amount of alcohol they consume, living upstairs from the bar has been an advantage.

Al's girlfriend, Anita Zito sits next to Eddie. Anita is a shapely, attractive brunette in her early thirties, who wears a nurse's uniform. Frankie and his friends all have the hots for her. She just got off her shift at Flushing Hospital. She and Al have been going out since high school and been talking about marriage for years. No one believes Al will ever do it. "Babe, why don't you close this place early tonight?" she asks Al.

Al looks around at the crowd and smiles at Anita. "Whatta ya got in mind?"

"Try to figure it out, big guy," she says seductively.

"I'm workin' on it." Al winks at her and refills her drink, and then works his way to the other end of the bar refilling glasses, and opening beer bottles as he goes. Charlie looks up at the Schaefer Beer clock over the bar.

Charlie catches Al's attention. "See, Al, I told ya they wouldn't be back by nine."

Al looks at the clock. "It ain't nine yet. If ya were so worried, ya should'a drove."

"Hey, don't start with me."

Al shrugs his shoulders in frustration, grabs a bottle of scotch from behind the bar, and pours a drink into Hanna's empty glass. "Thanks, Al," Hanna, says.

Angela looks at Charlie. "Where'd they go Charl?"

"They had to find somethin'."

"Stanzo go with them?" Maryanne asks.

"Who wants to know?"

Pinkie punches Charlie hard in the arm again.

"Ow! Hey, cut it out. You hurt."

"She wants to know."

"Don't fuck with me tonight."

"Hey, watch your language over there! There's ladies in the bar!" Eddie shouts.

"Sorry," Charlie says.

"Fuck 'em!" Buck, out of his semi-stupor, chimes in.

Al stands in front of Buck and points a finger in his face. "Hey, ya behave yourself! I don't want no trouble tonight, or I'll throw ya outta here on your ass again."

With head down and a sorrowful expression on his face, Buck says, "Sorry, Al." Buck adds to his apology by raising his glass in a toast. The others return the gesture and Buck drinks.

"God bless ya Buck," Hanna says.

Buck's head slumps further down as he returns to his partially conscious state.

"See what ya started, Charl. Ya gotta be such a prick. She just asked if Stanzo was with 'em," Angela says.

"It ain't my turn to watch him."

"Funny. You're a real scream Charlie Ferraro," Maryanne adds.

"Whatta ya so interested in Stanzo for?"

"Ya jerk! She's got a crush on him," Pinkie says.

Smiling, "Yeah, he's a cutie-pa-tootie," Maryanne says.

CHAPTER 6

Stanzo sits in a comfortable looking chair opposite Linda, who sits on her living room couch with its plastic seat covers. Twenty-one-year old Linda has olive skin, long black hair, green eyes, a knockout shape, and long shapely legs. She's an honor student, plays piano, and attends Queens College, majoring in music. While still a student at Queens College, Stanzo met Linda.

Her abusive father, Frank, a plumber, has a drinking problem. Her mother Mary, a housewife, suffers from her husband's abuse. Linda has two older brothers who have their own families. Linda wants to move out of the house as soon as possible. Her father doesn't like Stanzo, and Stanzo feels the same way about him.

"How come you can't go out again tonight?

"Benny, I just can't. I have a lot of homework."

"Oh, this is bullshit. Ya tell me to come over... Now ya can't go out..."

"Well at least we can see each other."

"Yeah, but I have a girlfriend who can't go out with me."

"Well maybe we should just stop seeing each other."

"Oh, that's what ya want?"

"I don't know. Well, maybe we should..."

"Fine!"

Linda's father, a short man with a potbelly, big round face, a red puffy nose, pencil thin mustache, and bad combover, enters the room.

"Ay, what are ya yellin' in my house for?"

"'Cause your daughter pisses me off"

"Yeah, well get the hell outta my house, then."

"Daddy, it's alright."

Stanzo steams. "That's the way ya want it?"

Before Linda answers, Frank grabs Stanzo forcefully by the arm. "Ya don't talk to my daughter that way."

Stanzo smells his booze breath and tries to wrestle his arm free. Frank's grip feels surprisingly strong.

"Daddy! Let him go!"

Stanzo and Frank scuffle a little, but then Frank releases Benny's arm and pushes him out of the living room.

"Ya son-of-a-bitch. Keep ya fuckin' hands off me!"

"Get the fuck out of my house."

"Daddy, leave him alone!" Linda screams.

The front door of the house opens and Frank pushes Stanzo out the door. He stumbles down the three front steps and almost topples over. Linda's father stands imposingly in the doorway with his arms across his chest. Stanzo grabs the open aluminum storm door and slams it in Frank's face. "Fuck you!" he shouts.

Pushing the door open, "I betta not see your fuckin' face around here again."

Stanzo struggles to control his anger. He stares at Linda's father just before the man slams the door shut. Stanzo walks away, stops, and then looks back at the door. He notices a large metal trash can in front of the house. He picks it up above his head and throws it with all his might at the aluminum storm door. It hits the door and the glass shatters. The can bounces off the inside door and tumbles down the steps.

The front door opens and Linda's father appears with a baseball bat in his hand. He starts down the steps after Stanzo who gives him the finger and disappears quickly around the corner. Frank, too slow to catch Stanzo, goes back into the house and slams the door.

CHAPTER 7

Charlie's Oldsmobile passes Al's bar. Inside the car, the guys have long, sad faces. Ricky says, "Hey, joo should park it down the block."

"Yeah, make 'em walk," Nicky adds.

They all laugh deviously as Frankie continues driving to the end of the street.

With dejection written all over his face, Frankie enters the bar; Nicky and Ricky follow. Charlie and the girls turn their attention towards the door. "It's about time!" Charlie says.

Frankie walks up to the bar and looks at Charlie. "What? Ya said nine! It's nine."

Nicky and Ricky join Frankie at the bar. "It's five after," Charlie says.

"Where's Stanzo?" Maryanne asks.

"We dropped him off in the Heights," Nicky tells her.

The girls share an understanding look. Maryanne's face shows a pang of jealousy. Frankie tosses Charlie's keys on the bar. "So, I take it you came up short?" Al asks.

"Al, we looked everywhere," Frankie says.

"Whatta ya lookin' for?" Pinkie asks innocently.

"Nothin'," Frankie says.

"They're probably looking for girls."

Frankie whispers in Angela's ear. She quickly moves her head away and stares at him but acts cool. Angela turns and whispers in Maryanne's ear. Maryanne's big brown eyes almost bug out of her head. "So where's Gloria tonight?" Angela asks with a hint of displeasure in her voice.

"Don't ask," Frankie says.

"She have too much fun at the Copa last night?" Pinkie asks. Frankie shows his surprise. "I talked to her today. She told me all about it. Some weekend—the Copa, Tony Bennett, an engagement ring. I love Tony Bennett. When ya gonna take us to the Copa?"

"Yeah, we'll all go some time," Frankie, says sincerely.

Charlie says, "Hey Maryanne, ya wanna go to the Copa?"

"Yeah, with Stanzo."

"No, I mean with me."

"You come into a large sum of money recently?"

"No, but I'm cute."

"That ain't gonna get us into the Copa."

Nicky catches Al's attention. "Give me a Johnny Walker Black on the rocks."

"So where'd ya look?" Al asks.

"Around here... Junction Boulevard, up the Heights—"

"Elmhurst, all over Corona..." Ricky adds.

"What makes you bright lights think anyone around here is gonna have a car like that? Ya gotta go to Flushing, Bayside, Forest Hills. Expensive neighborhoods. That's where you're gonna find one."

The guys look at each other remembering Stanzo's exact same words. "You corrupting these kids again?" Anita asks.

"Nah, I'm just consultin'."

With a smirk on her face, Anita says, "Yeah, right!"

"Maybe we'll go out again later," Frankie says.

Charlie downs his drink, picks up his change and keys, and turns to leave. "Not with my car, you ain't. See you gentlemen tomorrow night. Ya can fill me in on all the details."

"Thanks, Charl," Frankie says.

Charlie nods to Frankie and leaves. He stops at the door and turns around. "Hey Maryanne, you want a ride?"

"No thanks, Charl. I'm waiting for Stanzo."

"Oh, yeah. I forgot."

Charlie leaves.

Angela looks at Frankie and says, "Ya know why you're having accidents? Don't ya?"

"Because of Gloria?" Frankie asks.

Angela looks curiously at Frankie and says, "'Cause ya drive too fast."

"I gotta go call Gloria." Frankie heads for the phone booth.

Frankie tries Gloria's number several times and keeps getting a busy signal so he returns to the bar. He sits in Charlie's seat. "So ya gonna sit around here all night like a bunch of assholes and quitters?" Al asks.

"If these guys can help me straighten my fender and bumper, we can take my car and go out and look some more."

The front door swings open and an angry Charlie enters. "Okay wiseasses. Where's my fuckin' car?"

Buck's head pops up. "Hey, watch your language." In a trance-like state, his head immediately drops back down.

The guys laugh. "I'm not kiddin'. Where's my car?"

"Down the block. Joo didn't see it?" Ricky asks, barely holding back a smile.

Frankie sensing Charlie's frustration says, "It's in Tuffaro's parking lot."

Charlie shakes his head in disgust. The guys all laugh. "Funny!" Charlie turns around to leave and bumps into Stanzo. It distracts Stanzo from noticing Maryanne. Seeing him, her face lights up.

Al notices Stanzo. "Look what the wind blew in— another asshole quitter."

Stanzo walks up to the bar. "Don't start with me, Al! I told them where to go. They wouldn't listen."

"Hi, Benny!" Maryanne says timidly.

Stanzo notices her for the first time. "Hi!"

With a big smile on her face, Maryanne says, "I was hoping to see you. And here you are."

"Yeah," he answers, and looks for an empty stool far away from Maryanne but can't find one. He sits next to Anita. "Just don't break my balls tonight," he says to Maryanne.

"That's not nice," Anita says with a playful smile.

"Ya betta be nice to her, Stanzo," Angela says.

"Yeah!" Pinkie adds.

"Whatta ya her guardian angels?"

"Just be nice. That's all I'm sayin'," Angela says.

"I am nice. How are ya Maryanne?"

Maryanne brightens with a smile. "Fine."

Frankie asks, "See what he's drinkin', Al?"

From down the bar, Stanzo says, "Dewars and water, Al. Make it a double. I need one."

"You're in a hostile mood tonight. Girlfriend trouble?" Anita asks.

The girls ears perk up. "Yeah. How ya doin'?"

"Yeah, fine."

Frankie looks over at Stanzo as Al places the drink in front of Stanzo. "We're goin' out again! We're taking my car," Frankie says.

"Yeah?"

"Ya gonna go with them, Benny? Maryanne asks.

"Ah... Yeah," he answers hesitantly.

"I thought maybe you were gonna hang out here tonight."

Trying to be nice to Maryanne, "Nah, we got this thing to do."

"I know. Frankie, told us. It sounds dangerous."

Stanzo looks over to Frankie. "You told them?"

"Don't worry about us, Stanzo. We never ratted on anybody, especially you guys," Angela says.

"Yeah, right," Stanzo says.

Indignantly, Angela says, "That's right, Stanzo. We stuck by you guys through some tough shit."

Frankie tells Al, "One more round, Al, and then, we leave."

Al pours Frankie another drink and places it in front of him. Al looks seriously at the guys. "So you know where to go? Listen to Stanzo. He's the only one with any brains around here."

"Hey, I still think this is a stupid idea, and ya want my advice—forget it. But, if ya insist on doin' this, we ain't gonna find one around here."

"There ya go. He's right," Al says. He leans into the bar and speaks softly, just loud enough for the guys to hear. "Now, if you find one, don't speed or go through any lights. Just be cool and you won't get caught. Remember, only idiots who do stupid things get caught."

The drink seems to bolster Frankie's resolve. "Let's do it!" Frankie says.

The guys down their drinks and get ready to leave, except for Stanzo. Frankie looks over at him. "Ya comin', Stanzo?"

Stanzo looks at Maryanne and knows he should go. "Yeah!" He gets up and the guys start to leave.

Maryanne turns around to watch them. "Bye, Benny! Maybe I'll see you later."

Over his shoulder, he says, "Yeah, right."

CHAPTER 8

Frankie's Bonneville looks odd with only one headlight as it cruises slowly down Forest Hills' streets. From the looks of the upscale Caddies, Lincolns, and newer model cars, this looks like the type of area to find a car like Frankie's. Inside the car, they watch both sides of the street, but street after street they see nothing.

They find themselves driving around residential neighborhoods in Flushing with the same results. They look desperately out the windows—still no Pontiac.

Frankie gives up on Flushing and crosses into Bayside. Frankie thinks to himself, *the faster I drive the more territory we can cover, and the faster we'll get back to the bar. It's too late to call Gloria. I'll just pick her up in the morning and drive her into the city for work.*

Frankie returns to the present when Ricky says, "Slow down. Joo can't see nothin'."

Frankie ignores him and thinks, *we ain't gonna find another car like this. I hate goin' back and tellin' Al, though. Five more minutes—that's it.*

"I ain't goin' back to the bar if Maryanne's there," Stanzo says.

"Oh come on, man. We ain't givin' up already," Nicky says.

"I'm just gonna go to Lorenzo's tomorrow and get an estimate."

"Now, you're makin' sense. You don't need to go to jail," Stanzo says.

"Come on Stanzo. Ya heard what Al says. We're not gonna get caught," Nicky says.

Stanzo balks, "Oh, you know for sure we're not gonna get caught."

"Joo heard what Al says, 'Only assholes get caught.'"

"Let me tell you somethin' about Al. Sometimes he's full of shit. Don't take everything he says as absolute fact," Stanzo says.

"Ya wouldn't say that to his face," Nicky says.

"I'll tell him to his fuckin' face. I ain't afraid—and he knows it."

"Stop!" Ricky shouts.

Stanzo looks around. "What? We're just talkin'."

To Frankie, he says, "No, stop! Joo idiot. Slow down. I saw somthin' back there."

"Where?" Frankie asks.

Everyone looks around as Frankie applies the breaks and the car comes to a stop in the middle of the street.

"Back there." Ricky turns around and points back the way they just came.

They turn around to look as Frankie slowly backs down the street. At the corner of a peaceful intersection, there sits an exact duplicate of Frankie's car. They pull up next to it and everyone stares in amazement.

"I can't fucking believe it," Ricky says,

"Now wait a minute. Let's think about this," Stanzo says.

Frankie pulls around the corner and parks on a dark, quiet street. He turns the lights and the car off. They all stare back at the other car. "Come on. Let's get out of here before someone sees us," Stanzo says.

"Joo crazy? After looking all night joo want to leave," Rick says.

"I ain't goin' to jail," Stanzo says.

"See man. It's a miracle," Nicky says with a big smile on his face.

Stanzo says to Frankie, "Don't listen to this asshole. He'll do anything crazy."

Frankie thinks to himself, *I know Stanzo's right, but I can't leave now. I'm too scared to move. I wonder if the other guys are as scared as I am.* He glances over at his friends. They all seem caught up in their own thoughts, and no one says anything.

"Come on. If we're gonna do it, let's do it now. We're wasting time," Ricky says.

"Yeah, he's right. I'm gonna take a look," Nicky says.

"Wait a minute," Stanzo tells him and Nicky stops. "Check out the neighborhood first." They all look in different directions. "If ya see anybody looking, just keep walking. We'll pick you up at that other corner."

"Okay." Stanzo opens the door, slides over as Nicky jumps out of the car and walks nonchalantly towards the other one. Inside Frankie's car, they watch Nicky. He tries to open the passenger door. "That asshole. What does he think, they were gonna leave it open for us?" Stanzo says.

"Joo shut up man."

"Fuck you. When he gets back we're gettin' out of here," Stanzo says.

"Shut up both of ya!" Frankie says as he watches Nicky in the rear view mirror. Nicky saunters around the back of the other car and over to the driver's side door. Frankie quickly snaps his head around when he sees the interior light of the other car come on as Nicky opens the driver's side door and quickly jumps in. His head disappears under the dash. "The door's open!" Frankie says.

"See," Ricky says.

Stanzo looks at Ricky. "See, shit! I don't like this. We're in the shit now."

Frankie asks, "What's he doin?"

"He's probably trying to get it started."

"Just keep your eyes on the street," Stanzo says.

They watch as Nicky's head reappears. He looks around the neighborhood, exits the car, runs back to Frankie's car, and gets in. Almost out of breath with excitement, he says, "I couldn't believe the door was open. I think I can hot-wire it. Someone has to hold a flashlight."

"I can do it," Ricky says.

"Anybody see ya?" Stanzo asks.

"I don't think so."

"Joo got a flashlight?" Ricky asks Frankie.

"And a screwdriver," Nicky says.

Frankie reaches into the glove box and pulls out a flashlight and screwdriver. Before he hands them over, he says, "Maybe we oughta think about this."

"Think about it—" Stanzo says.

"Oh, no. Don't get him going again," Ricky says.

"Fuckin' think about it! That's what I've been tryin' to tell ya. We're in the shit here. You know what happens—we get caught? How many years in jail we're looking at? Let's just get out of here, before somebody sees us," Stanzo says.

"Come on man. We found the car. We ain't gonna get caught. Come on Ricky," Nicky says.

Nicky and Ricky look around before they get out. They walk quickly to the other Bonneville. Nicky gets in the driver's side and unlocks the passenger door. Ricky opens it and jumps in.

Stanzo sulks and says, "Nobody wants to listen to me."

"Just keep your eyes open. I'll watch this street—you watch the other," Frankie says.

"Yeah, don't worry about me."

In the other car, Nicky and Ricky disappear under the dash; the flashlight illuminates the inside of the car.

"Geez... that light's too bright. Oh man someone's gonna see them," Stanzo says.

"Take it easy. It's late, nobody's gonna see us. Just keep your eyes on the street."

"It's already taking too long. They should'a had it started. He's full of shit. He doesn't know how to hot-wire it."

"Hey, man, give them a chance."

"I'm gonna go see what's goin' on."

Stanzo starts to get out of the car. Frankie grabs his arm. "Just hold still." Just then, the flashlight goes out in the other car. Nicky and Ricky's heads pop up, and they get out of the car. They look around as they walk fast to Frankie's car. Ricky gets in the back seat; Nicky squeezes in next to Stanzo. "There's some kind of plate over the ignition wires. I can't get to them," Nicky says.

"Ok, that's it—let's get out of here," Stanzo says.

Frankie shakes his head, no. "We found the car. What are we gonna do—leave it?"

"We're here too long. Somebody's gonna see us and call the cops," Stanzo says.

Frankie looks at his watch, "It's one o'clock. Everyone's sleeping."

"I ain't leavin' now," Nicky says.

"Joo want to tell Al we found a car and couldn't get it started?"

"Fuck Al. We could get caught," Stanzo says.

Nicky says, "You got some pliers?"

"Look in the glove compartment," Frankie says.

Nicky rifles through the glove box.

"Look, let's just forget it and go home," Stanzo says desperately.

Nicky moves things around in the cramped glove box. "I don't see any pliers."

"We betta get out of here if we don't do somethin' quick," Stanzo says.

Frankie looks at all of them, "Any ideas?"

"I'll go back and try to get through that plate. I know I can get it started once I do," Nicky says.

Stanzo rolls his eyes. Deep in their own thoughts, a silence falls over them. Finally, Stanzo breaks the quiet, "Why don't you try Frankie's key?"

They laugh. "That's right, assholes. Laugh. Ya gonna sit here all night? My old man locked his keys in the car at the cemetery once and they were closing. Another Chevy came along. My old man stopped him.

They tried the guy's key, and bingo—it opened the door."

"No shit?" Ricky asks.

"It might work. There aren't that many keys," Nicky says.

"Let's try it," Ricky says.

Frankie pulls his key out of the ignition and hands it to Nicky.

"And don't take your sweet ass time. If it doesn't work, we get the hell out of here," Stanzo says.

Nicky looks at Stanzo with contempt. "You wanna go with me?" he asks.

"No."

"Then shut the fuck up."

Nicky opens the door, gets out, looks around, walks to the other Pontiac, and gets in. Nicky settles into the driver's seat, and inserts the key in the ignition. He pumps the gas pedal, turns the key. The big engine turns over and purrs just like Frankie's. Nicky's face lights with excitement. Frankie and Ricky cheer. A not so jubilant Stanzo looks glum.

With adrenalin pumping and a wide grin on his face, Nicky puts the car in drive. It pulls forward, swings around the corner and parks in front of Frankie's car. Nicky leaves the car running and pulls Frankie's key out of the ignition. He gets out of the car, walks back to Frankie's car and sticks his head into Frankie's open window. "You're a fuckin' genius Stanzo." He hands Frankie back his key.

Stanzo replies, "Put it back where ya got it and let's get outta here before someone sees us."

"Yeah, right," Nicky says.

"Who gives a fuck—we just committed grand theft auto," Frankie says.

"Ay, he's right. Joo betta get outta here," Ricky says.

Nicky asks Frankie, "Where ya wanna take it?"

"To my garage. Who's gonna drive it?"

"Me. I got it started," Nicky says, not expecting anything less.

Stanzo frowns at Nicky. "You don't even have a license!"

"I go with him," Ricky says.

"We can't drive back the same way. Somebody spots two cars like this and this one banged-up, they're gonna suspect something," Stanzo says.

"We'll meet at the garage," Nicky says.

"And don't let it stall. You might not be able to get it started, again. And if it does, just leave it and get the fuck outta there!" Stanzo warns.

Ricky climbs out of the car. He and Nicky walk to the stolen car. Frankie and Stanzo watch as the other Pontiac drives away.

At the next corner, Nicky makes a right onto the main street and disappears.

Frankie starts his car while Stanzo looks out the window to see if anyone has seen them. "Okay?" Frankie asks.

"Yeah, but go straight for a few blocks. I hope they make it back to Corona without getting stopped. That asshole doesn't even have a license. This is crazy... we're gonna get in a lot of shit for this."

CHAPTER 9

Later that night, Al tidies up around the bar in anticipation of closing. Most of the regulars have gone for the night, only Buck remains with his head on top of the bar and resting on his arms. Al looks at the front door when he hears voices.

Frankie, Ricky, and Nicky walk through the door. They scan the bar to see if Maryanne has left, then signal Stanzo to enter. He looks uncertain as he comes through the door and does a quick check of his own. As they sit down at the bar, Al senses their excitement. "If it ain't the cats that swallowed the canaries," Al says.

"That Maryanne gone?" Stanzo asks.

"No, she's behind the bar here givin' me a blowjob."

"Give us a round, Al," Frankie says, throwing a bill on the bar.

"So what did ya find?"

"Man, joo not gonna believe it." Ricky says.

"Al, it was a piece of cake. It was easier than I thought," Nicky says.

Frankie adds, "Listen to this, Al. Same exact car. Same year, white, convertible, black interior, black leather seats."

"No..."

"Yeah, only difference—the seats are powered and it's got spoke wheels. We're gonna put the seats in my car and put on the wheels. Oh yeah, and it has a better radio, too. We're putting that in too."

Al finishes pouring drinks and pushes Frankie's money away. "This ones on me. So how'd you get in?"

"The door was open," Nicky says.

"Joo tell him how we got it started?" Ricky asks.

"With Frankie's key," Nicky says.

"No! It's one in a million. How'd you ever figga to use his key. I probably wouldn't a thought of it myself."

"Yeah, they'd still be out there if it wasn't for me," Stanzo says.

Al shakes his head, playfully smacks Stanzo's cheek, reaches out and shakes his hand. "Stanzo, you're goin' places in this world."

Stanzo laughs. "Yeah, straight to Sing Sing with these schmucks."

"Not if you're smart and get rid of it right away. Don't sweat it. Anybody see ya?"

"I don't think so. It was a pretty deserted neighborhood," Frankie says.

"That's good. Where is it?"

"The car?" Frankie asks.

"Yeah."

"In my garage."

"When ya gonna fix it?"

"Tomorrow morning, early. Maybe eight."

"Are you crazy... eight? I'm just gettin' to bed at eight," Nicky says.

"I gotta go to work tomorrow. Monday's a busy day," Stanzo says.

"I'll be there man. I'll take the day off," Ricky offers.

"Good. We'll meet at the garage," Frankie says.

Al advises, "And don't let too many people see what you're doin'."

"Nobody's around during the day."

Al looks at Frankie and says, "And I would suggest that you don't let that girlfriend of yours come around."

"She's at work all day." It reminds him that he didn't call Gloria, and now, he won't be able to drive her to work in the morning, either.

Al says, "It's gonna be easy. Ya just need some ratchets. You take that fender off one-two-three. It's a new car so there shouldn't be any rust to deal with. Ya get the bumper and the grill off. Ya only got a few screws on those headlights. Ya got tools?"

"I'll bring my tool box," Ricky says.

"I'll bring my old man's tools," Nicky adds.

"You're lucky ya don't have to change the hood. They're a bitch to line up." Al pours drinks and places them in front of the guys. Al raises his own glass and says, *"Chin Don."*

They all raise their glasses and clink. Stanzo downs his drink. "Well I'm gettin' outta here. I'll see you tomorrow night," pointing a finger at them, "and be careful. I don't wanna read about you in the papers."

"If everyone stays cool and ya dump it as soon as you're finished, no one's gonna get caught. Remember, only assholes who do stupid things get caught."

"Hey Al, ya keep saying that, but I'm still worried."

"Don't do anything stupid and ya won't have to worry." Stanzo makes a disparaging face.

They say good-bye to Stanzo. As he walks towards the door, Frankie calls to him: "Stanzo!"

Stanzo stops and turns around. "Yeah?"

"Thanks!"

"Yeah, man. Just be careful."

They watch him leave.

"I'm goin' home, too," Ricky says.

"Me, too," Nicky says.

They get up and Frankie says, "I'll drop you guys off."

Al reminds them, "Stanzo's right. Be careful tomorrow. And don't tell too many people about this."

"Okay, goodnight, Al," Frankie says.

As they're walking out the door, Nicky says, "Hey man, can't we do this at maybe two o'clock."

CHAPTER 10

Frankie has a garage around the corner behind someone else's house. Not all the houses in the neighborhood have garages. Frankie rents one of four garages behind a two family house.

The next morning, Frankie's car sits in front of the open garage doors. The stolen car, looking pristine and shiny, waits in the garage. While sipping coffee from paper cups and smoking cigarettes, Ricky, Nicky and Frankie examine the damage to Frankie's car.

"Hey, man it don't look so bad today," Ricky says as he gets up, goes over to Frankie's car, and lifts the hood.

A bedraggled-looking Nicky says, "Let's start on your car. I still don't know why we couldn't do it at two."

"I gotta drive the old man to work at four," Frankie says.

Ricky opens a large toolbox, takes out a long socket wrench handle, and fits it with a socket. Nicky looks under the hood, and says, "There's six bolts here," pointing to the bolts securing the fender. "The others we'll have to get from underneath."

"I'll start on the other car," Frankie says as he picks out a socket wrench and goes into the garage.

"And I'll get this bumper off," Nicky says. He crawls under the car with an open-ended wrench in his hand and starts to undo the bolts holding the bumper.

Later in the afternoon, Frankie's car has gone through a transformation. It has a new fender and bumper as well as the spoke wheels. Frankie sits inside the car playing with his new power seats. He moves them forward, backward, then up and down. The guys stand next to the car. "I love these seats," Frankie says. He turns the knob on the radio and they hear a newscaster say, "…In Vietnam news, U.S. Marine units participating in Operation Starlight encountered and attacked Vietcong guerrillas around Chu Lai." Frankie changes the station. "Dancing in the Street" by Martha and the Vandellas blasts out of the radio.

"Whoa! Cool radio," Nicky says.

"Yeah, it's stereo," Frankie, says.

Frankie turns off the radio then the engine. He gets out of the car, takes a Marlboro box out of his shirt pocket, opens it, removes a cigarette, and offers his friends, who each take one. They walk over and sit on top of some old tires, smoking their cigarettes and admiring their work. "Looks great," Nicky, says.

"Joor old man's never gonna know joo had an accident."

"Hey man, I can't believe we got those seats, the radio and wheels done too," Frankie says.

Frankie's landlord, a big man in his early sixties wearing hunting garb, comes out his back door and says, "Hey, where'd ya steal that one?"

Frankie flushes red. Nicky and Ricky shift uncomfortably and stare at Frankie, who tries to force a laugh and compose himself. Frankie says, "Ah... My friend got drafted. Yeah... He got drafted and sold me his car when he heard I had an accident. We used it for parts."

Nicky and Ricky look at him wondering why he told the landlord so much.

Frankie looks uncomfortable, and wonders, *why did I tell this guy all that. Maybe he'll say something to my old man."*

"That's good. Looks just like yours."

"Yeah, I'm gonna be gettin' rid of it soon.

"Ya'd never know it was in an accident.

"Yeah, it turned out alright."

"How's your father?"

"Good... Yeah... Good." Frankie answers nervously.

"Tell him I said hello."

"I will."

"You think you're gonna get drafted, too?"

"I'm hopin' to get married. But who knows."

"Oh, yeah. My nephew, Eddie, got his notice last week. This damn thing is gonna wind up another Korea. I was in the Navy in the Pacific myself in World War II. Did I show ya where I got hit?" He starts to lift his shirt. Frankie quickly motions he has seen it and the landlord stops. "Ya never knew when you were coming home. Well listen, good luck! Hope you don't get drafted. If you do, never volunteer for nothin'. That's what they always told me. My nephew will probably go to basic at Fort Dix. You can at least get home on weekends."

Frankie laughs. "Yeah, dicks, they got a lot of them there."

The landlord either doesn't get Frankie's attempt at humor or chooses to ignore it. "That's if they don't send ya over there. Well I gotta take a shower. We was duck huntin' out on the Island this weekend. See ya!" He turns and goes in the house.

"He's a pleasant guy," Nicky says.

"Joo think he believes joo about the car?"

"Yeah. He's got no reason not to. But we gotta get rid of this thing tonight." Frankie looks at his watch. "Hey, I gotta split. Can you guys clean up and close the garage?"

"Yeah, we'll take care of it," Nicky says.

"I'll see ya tonight" Frankie climbs in his newly restored car, starts it, cranks up the radio volume, and backs out of the driveway. He hears the radio newscaster say, "It has been reported that communist troop numbers have risen from their 1963 totals of 30,000—" Frankie fiddles with the dial until he finds a rock and roll station and Dion and the Belmonts', "A Teenager in Love," plays.

Frankie comes out of his house wearing his restaurant clothes—black pants, a white shirt, black bow tie, and he carries a black tuxedo jacket over his arm. His father dresses similarly wearing his jacket and black fedora. Albert locks the front door, and follows Frankie to the car and they get in. Frankie starts the car and fiddles with the seat controls, adjusting the power seats, and turns on the radio to hear a newscaster say, "...Marines patrolling the air base at Chu Lai were involved in heavy fighting today—" Frankie pushes one of the radio's buttons to a music channel.

As Frankie fiddles with the power seats Albert asks, "These new?"

"Yeah, I just got 'em." Frankie hates lying to his father but rationalizes—he did just get them.

"Yeah? They're nice."

Frankie's glad his father approves and that he has no idea about the accident. *I still can't believe it went so easy. The sooner we get rid of it, the better I'll feel.*

"Gloria called. She said she didn't hear from you."

"Yeah, I forgot to call her last night."

"Didn't ya go out last night?"

"Nah, she wasn't feeling well. So... So I gave her the ring and left." Frankie starts the car and pulls away from the curb.

"Oh, that's too bad. She didn't say anything about that. She did say to come over tonight."

"Thanks, Pop."

"Yeah, I hope things work out with you two."

Frankie glances over at his father thinking—*yeah, me too.*

That night at Russo's Restaurant, the after-work and pre-theater crowd keep the place busy. The restaurant looks like the typical Italian joint with red and white tablecloths, empty Chianti bottles with candle drippings down the sides on every table, and dark wood café chairs around tables. The wall on the other side of the room has semi-circular red booths. The restaurant has a kitchen in the rear, and a long dark wood bar on one side with tables and booths opposite the bar.

Frankie scurries about, helping bussers clean and re-set tables for the next seating. His father helps behind the bar, mixing drinks and chatting with customers. Frankie seats an attractive couple. He stops at one of the booths before returning to the front. "Hello Mr. Cavanaugh! How are you tonight?"

Cavanaugh, a well-known attorney in his forties, entertains clients several nights a week at the restaurant. Tonight, he sits with two businessmen. "We're fine."

"Have you ordered yet?"

"No we haven't. Do you have any recommendations, Frankie?"

"We have a nice steak Florentine tonight. It comes with a side of ravioli. And the blue fish is fresh. We can prepare it anyway you like."

Cavanaugh looks at his guests and says, "Frankie's recommendations are always the best." They look up from their menus and smile at Frankie.

"Thank you, Frankie."

Frankie looks down at their empty martini glasses and asks, "Another round?"

Cavanaugh looks at his guests, who shake their heads in agreement. Cavanaugh nods to Frankie to bring them another round.

"We'll get that for you right away."Frankie heads to the bar and places the order. On his way back to the front, the actor Don Ameche stops him. He sits across from a man with gray hair that Frankie knows to be a Broadway producer. "So Frankie, are you worried about the draft?" Ameche asks.

"Yeah, a little. I'm hoping to get married before they draft me."

"I hope you have a girlfriend. You need one to get married." Ameche laughs.

Frankie laughs, too. "Yeah, I do. I just proposed to her the other night."

Ameche puts out his hand and Frankie shakes it. "Well congratulations on that. It sounds a lot better than going to Vietnam."

"Thanks. I think so too. Can I get you anything else?"

"No, we're stuffed as usual. The Veal Marsala was excellent tonight."

"Glad you enjoyed it. Just let us know if you need anything else."

"Maybe an espresso in a little while."

"Sure. Can I bring you a dessert menu?"

"We're stuffed but we'll take a look."

"I'll get you some menus."

"Thanks."

Frankie moves away and heads for the front after stopping to chat with several other customers.

Later that night at the local lover's lane, Frankie and Gloria make love in the back seat of the Pontiac. Gloria, with an open blouse and no bra, moans softly as Frankie caresses and kisses her firm breasts. "Stop! Stop! I can't do this tonight."

"What? You on the rag?"

"Frankie..."

"What?

"I just can't. I gotta get home. I have to go to work in the morning."

Frankie kisses her lips and whispers, "Just a little longer."

Gloria, caught up in the moment, throws her head back and sighs, but then much to Frankie's surprise she pulls away and starts to straighten her clothing. "I gotta go."

"But we just made up."

"I know. I love you." She kisses him gently on the lips.

"I love you too."

Gloria reaches around Frankie's neck, and the diamond engagement ring gleams in the partial light. She kisses him passionately. They throw their arms tightly around each other and start to make love again.

CHAPTER 11

Early evening at the bar finds Al busy putting bottles of beer into the ice tub. Buck, with his head still erect, sits in his usual seat. Frankie, Ricky, and Nicky nurse beers as they stare at the TV and the newscaster says, "In fighting in Vietnam, a Viet Cong battalion wiped out an ARVN relief force twenty miles north of Saigon. Fifty-four ARVN troops were killed and wounded. A U.S. miltary spokesman referring to the incident was quoted as saying, 'We make the same mistake all the time.'"

"Look at this shit. The guy has no arm left. It makes me sick. Little gooks in pajamas kickin' ass. It's disgusting... This is the goddamn United States of America. We're gonna lose this war they keep this shit up," Al says.

From the end of the bar, Buck says, "America never lost a war!"

They all look over at Buck. "Yeah, what about Korea?" Nicky asks.

"That wasn't no war. It was a Police Action," Buck answers.

Wiping the bar top, Al says, "Police Action my ass! It was a war just like this one. When you send troops half way around the world—it's a war. It's stupid politicians making money off the whole damn thing."

"Ah, you're full'a shit. I'd go fight if they asked me."

"Don't joo worry Buck, they ain't askin' joo."

Stanzo enters cautiously, looking towards the back room. "Mayanne here?"

Al looks down and says, "Hey, Maryanne quit suckin' me. Stanzo's here."

"Funny. You wish you could get a blowjob."

"I got you when I need one." Stanzo smirks at Al as he sits on a bar stool. "Whatta ya wanna drink?"

"Gimme me a Black Label rocks." Stanzo looks at his friends. "Everything go okay?"

"Yeah. Didn't ya see the car? It's right outside," Frankie says.

"Yeah, it looks good."

"Nothing to it," Nicky says.

"We gotta get rid of it tonight," Frankie says.

"Hey, Stanzo! Ya think Vietnam is a war or a Police Action?" Buck asks.

Stanzo turns his attention to Buck. "It's a pain in the ass."

"Ya can say that again."

The guys turn around when they hear voices outside. The door opens. And to Stanzo's disappointment, Maryanne comes through the door followed by Pinkie, Angela, and a new girl who catches all their attention. At about five-feet-four, with shapely legs and beautiful brown hair that hangs around her shoulders, she looks Latin and exudes sensuality. She wears a green clingy cotton blouse and tight white pants.

Maryanne walks directly to Stanzo and sits next to him. "Hi Benny. How are you tonight?"

Stanzo stares at the new girl. "Not good Maryanne..."

"I heard there was a little trouble up the Heights last night."

"Yeah, Stanzo, didn't ya parents tell ya not to throw garbage cans?" Pinkie says.

With puzzling expressions, Stanzo's friends look to him for an explanation. "I had a fight with Linda and her old man came after me with a baseball bat."

"What?" Frankie says.

Nicky jumps off his stool. "Son-of-a-bitch. Let's go kick his ass."

Ricky grabs Nicky by the arm. "Whoa... hold it..."

"I'll get that son-of-a-bitch. He'll get a bat in the back of his head some night when he's comin' home with a half a bag on. He's the reason she broke up with me."

A broad smile crosses Maryanne's face when she hears the words "broke up."

"I know he's been puttin' this shit in her head about me."

"Yeah, well you're gonna start a lot of trouble. Didn't ya mother tell ya not to throw garbage cans when ya were a little kid?" Angela asks.

"Funny," Stanzo says.

Al and the guys laugh at this. All the while Stanzo has been watching the new girl as she slithers up on the bar stool next to Maryanne. The other two girls sit next to her.

Stanzo stares at the way her sumptuous breasts caress the edge of the bar. Pinkie says, "Hey everybody, this is Priscilla." She points to each of the guys. "Frankie... Nicky... Ricky... Stanzo..." She points to Al. "And this is Al."

Priscilla's dark beauty and sultriness attracts Al's attention, too. He reaches over the bar takes her hand and kisses the back of it. The guys notice the gesture and whoop.

"*Chan tay...* pretty lady," Al coos.

In a throaty, sexy voice with complete composure, Priscilla says, "Nice to meet you, Al. Nice to meet all of you."

"Priscilla came here from Puerto Rico when she was little. She moved here last year from the Bronx. She's in one of my beauty culture classes," Pinkie adds.

"What can I get for you ladies?" Al asks.

The girls order their favorite drinks and Al prepares them. "I'll have a coke, Al... with two cherries, please," Priscilla says.

Al smiles. "Certainly!"

Maryanne watches with envy as Stanzo turns his attention past her towards Priscilla. "It's incredible we never met before," he says.

"Whatta ya mean?"

"I feel this unbelievable magnetism to you."

Priscilla looks flattered. "You do?"

As Maryanne listens, her face registers apprehension.

"Yeah, I felt it as soon as ya came in."

With a playful smile on her face, Priscilla asks, "What's this about garbage cans?

"I like to throw them."

"You a garbage man?"

"No, I have a bad temper."

"Oh, I don't want to get you mad then." She smiles.

Maryanne's head swivels back and forth between the two. She obviously doesn't like the way things are going and feels uncomfortable sitting there.

"So, ya have a boyfriend?" Stanzo asks.

"I might. You have a girlfriend?"

"Not anymore."

Maryanne fumes, suddenly jumps up, and runs to the ladies' room in the back. Angela and Pinkie notice and run after her. Stanzo hardly notices what's going on, but Priscilla does. Stanzo slides into Maryanne's seat. "I think she likes you," Priscilla says.

"Yeah, I know. You might have a boyfriend. So does that mean you do or you don't?"

"I might."

"So you're mysterious?"

"You think so?"

"Yeah."

Just then, Charlie walks through the front door. Everybody turns to look at him. Several of them say, "Hi!" Charlie stops when he notices Priscilla.

Charlie walks over to Stanzo, all the while staring at Priscilla "Hey Stanzo, I was just up the Heights. There's a lot of pissed people up there." Angela returns from the ladies' room and hears Charlie's warning.

"Yeah, well that's tough shit."

"JoJo says to tell ya to stay out of the Heights if ya know what's good for ya."

"Don't say I didn't tell ya so," Angela chimes in.

"Fuck him!" Stanzo says.

"Hey, I'm just the messenger." Charlie grins at Priscilla who smiles back in her very seductive way. "Who's your friend? Charlie asks.

"This is Priscilla." To Priscilla he says, "This is Charlie."

Flirtatiously she says, "Hi!"

Maryanne and Pinkie return from the ladies' room. Maryanne's eyes look puffy and red.

Charlie stares playfully at Priscilla, and then turns his attention back to Stanzo. "Hey, no shit. JoJo says, 'Tell your friend Stanzo he better keep his ass out of the Heights.'"

"That prick said that?"

"I swear."

"Hey, ya hear this shit?" Fuckin' JoJo says, "I better stay out of the Heights."

Al suggests, "Maybe you should."

Nicky stands, walks over to Stanzo and Charlie. "That fuck. Let's go kick his ass," Nicky says.

"Benny, he's Linda's cousin," Angela says.

"Hey, I don't know if we wanna start with those crazy fucks. That JoJo's a nut job," Frankie says from where he's sitting.

"Let's just go up there and see what he's got to say. If he's got a problem, let him tell me to my face."

Maryanne says sweetly, "Ya better be careful, Benny."

Stanzo casts a discomforting look in her direction. Maryanne shifts uncomfortably and keeps her mouth shut. They gather their change and down their drinks. "Hey!" Al points a finger at them. "Watch your step with JoJo."

"Al, we're just gonna talk to him," Stanzo says.

"Yeah, that's how it starts. Just use your heads. You're walking onto his turf. And I don't want them in here causing trouble, either."

Priscilla grabs Stanzo's arm and stops him. "I want to come."

He looks at her with a how-do-I-say-no-look. "Yeah, sure."

Priscilla hops off the stool, Maryanne and the other girls watch them leave. Maryanne says, "Maybe I should'a gone with him…"

CHAPTER 12

The guys and Priscilla get out of Frankie and Charlie's cars in Corona Heights, about twelve blocks from Al's. They call this part of Corona the Heights, probably because you go up a hill to get there, and it overlooks the rest of Corona.

Mikey's Pool Hall sits on the ground floor of a two-story gray-shingled house. Next to the entrance, a wide glass window with a neon Rheingold sign hangs in the middle.

All the tough guys in the Heights hang out at Mikey's. Some people still refer to them as "The Heights Boys," their old street gang name. Marriages and families haven't kept these guys from hanging out together.

Stanzo opens the front door. Priscilla walks in beside him, and his friends follow. A Yankee game plays on the TV. Mel Allen, the announcer, says, "The Yankees lead the Indians three to nothing at the end of five." Sensing trouble, some heads at the bar, just to the right of the door turn their attention away from the game. They take note of the intruders. In a joint like this, you don't know who you'll have to fight.

Stanzo and his entourage continue towards the back where a number of guys stand around the six pool tables shooting pool. Others sit on benches around the back and side walls of the dimly lit area. They watch Stanzo and his friends boldly enter their domain. Priscilla in her skintight white pants attracts the most attention. Stanzo and the guys quickly size things up. JoJo and his friends have the odds on their side, but that doesn't deter Stanzo.

The room gets most of its light from fluorescent fixtures hanging several feet above the tables' surfaces. Stanzo walks over to JoJo at one of the middle tables as JoJo lines up a shot. Stanzo's friends follow him. JoJo, about to shoot, stops, and looks up at Stanzo. He turns back to realign the shot with the kind of cocky confidence that allows him to turn his back on danger. JoJo in his middle-twenties has greasy curly black hair, and despite a lazy right eye, looks ruggedly handsome.

As he shoots, his muscular forearm and bicep flex, and then relax. He wears a black t-shirt that accentuates his muscular chest; a pack of Lucky Strikes sticks out from under the t-shirt sleeve. Stanzo looks down at JoJo, still leaning over the table watching the ball he hit fall into the pocket. "I hear I'm supposed to stay out of the Heights."

Without looking up, JoJo replies, "Mister Stanzo! I'm glad to hear news travels fast around here."

"Yeah, it sure does."

Nicky grabs a pool cue from a rack, turns it around so that the fat end faces out and readies himself to do some damage as he makes his way to Stanzo's side. JoJo's boys notice Nicky's aggressive action and arrogant look and begin to surround the intruders. The tension in the room thickens. JoJo's guys tighten their circle around Stanzo and his friends. "He can come to the Heights any time he wants!" Nicky says threateningly.

Nicky's tone grabs the attention of those still sitting. They get to their feet and grab pool cues. JoJo straightens up and levels his eyes menacingly at Nicky. Play stops at all tables and a silence falls over the room.

"Is that right, Nicky? He can come to the Heights if he knows how to behave in the Heights. When he starts actin' like a '*Gavon*' and threatens my family members, he better watch out."

Stanzo looks JoJo squarely in the eye. "Your family's the problem."

"You're treadin' on very dangerous water now."

Stanzo shrewdly looks around the room. "We'll see about that."

"Stay out of the Heights!" JoJo warns.

Stanzo moves a step closer to JoJo and stares him in the face. "I'm comin' up here any time I want."

JoJo looks around at his boys, who ready themselves to stomp these guys upon his command. Frankie, Ricky, and Charlie shift uncomfortably. During the exchange, Priscilla watches Stanzo and his cool demeanor.

"This one is a social visit. Next time, it's your ass."

Stanzo holds his gaze on JoJo. "We'll see!" From his wide stance and fists at the ready, Stanzo obviously plans to test JoJo's threat.

A deadly silence falls over the room with only the drone of the ballgame filling the air. The folks sitting at the bar in front turn their attention towards the rear as well. Stanzo and JoJo hold each other's threatening gaze. Without dropping his eyes, Stanzo grabs Priscilla's arm and backs away slowly. His friends back up too. A little pushing and shoving takes place as Stanzo's friends break through the tight circle around them.

The intruders make their way to the front door. JoJo and his boys hold their places. Frankie and his friends get to the door; Nicky arrogantly tosses his pool cue on the floor, making a loud, disturbing racket. Some of the people at the bar react to the bouncing cue stick with angry faces. They watch Frankie and crew exit.

Once the front door closes, JoJo turns his attention back to his pool game as if the incident never took place.

Priscilla and the guys get in the cars, knowing they must deal with JoJo again.

CHAPTER 13

A little later the same night, Stanzo and the guys return to Al's Bar. Stanzo walks in with Priscilla on his arm, and the others follow. Maryanne eyes Stanzo and Priscilla enviously. As they approach the bar, Al says, "How'd it go?"

"That JoJo's gonna catch a beatin'... I hate that guy," Nicky says.

"He thinks everything that goes on in the Heights is his business," Frankie says.

"No, he makes it his business," Stanzo adds.

"Well he's a crazy fuck. So just watch what ya say to him." Al also knows that it isn't over with JoJo.

Everyone takes seats at the bar. "Joo think they'll draft his fuckin' ass?" Ricky asks. They all laugh at the thought of JoJo in the army.

"Hey, wouldn't that be funny. Shit. They take him—this country's really in trouble," Nicky says.

Buck's head pops up. "We're already in trouble." Everyone looks over at him and watches as his head slowly sinks back down.

Priscilla coos to Stanzo, "You were really cool."

Under her breath, Maryanne says sarcastically, "Yeah, he's cool."

Priscilla throws her head back, flaunts her luxurious hair and says to Stanzo, "I have to go home. Can you walk me?"

"Yeah. I'll walk ya," Stanzo volunteers.

She smiles at him. "Okay." They both stand up. "Goodnight everybody. It was fun meeting all of you. Thanks for letting me hang out."

"Goodnight, Benny," Maryanne says.

"Yeah, goodnight," Stanzo says over his shoulder.

Stanzo and Priscilla leave. Maryanne bursts into tears and runs to the ladies' room again. The girls follow her. The guys have seen this before; they pay little attention. Frankie picks up his cigarettes from the bar and his change. "I'm goin' too." He looks at Nicky and Ricky and tells them, "We'll get rid of that thing tomorrow night."

Nicky and Ricky nod in agreement.

Priscilla presses close to Stanzo, her arm tightly in his as they walk down the street. "This is it," Priscilla says.

They stop in front of a two-story white house with a front porch, just a few blocks from Al's. Priscilla puts her arms around Stanzo's neck and pulls his face to her. She kisses him passionately, pushing her tongue into his mouth. At first, Stanzo shifts uncomfortably, not accustomed to a girl this aggressive. The kiss lasts a long moment and completely absorbs Stanzo's entire being.

As soon as they separate, Priscilla turns and runs up the steps into the house, leaving Stanzo standing there trying to regain his composure. A smile crosses his face as he stares at the front door, and wonders how he got lucky enough to meet Priscilla.

CHAPTER 14

Several days later, Frankie still has the stolen car in his garage. It has gotten busy enough at Al's that Eddie Callahan helps Al behind the bar. On nights like this, he usually gives Al a hand in exchange for free drinks. The regulars sit in their usual places at the bar. Al and Eddie keep everyone happy by refreshing their drinks.

Al stands in front of Frankie and tells him, "Just strip it and sell the parts."

"I don't know... It sounds risky. I don't want it around too long. We should have got rid of it by now."

Nicky jumps into the conversation. "Man, I can sure use the bread. It'll keep my old man off my back about getting a job. The only time he bugs me is when I ask him for money."

"Yeah, we could sell the engine and tranie, the wheels, even..." Ricky says.

Nicky leans closer to Frankie. "Yeah, man. See how easy it is to strip. We can get it all taken apart in no time."

"Yeah, then joo just get an acetylene torch and cut it up. By the time joo get through with it, joo just throw the rest in a garbage can, man."

Frankie looks doubtful. "I don't know. Let me think about it."

Stanzo sits on the other side of Frankie and says, "What are ya fuckin' crazy?"

"There's a lot of guys around here would buy that shit. Right Al?" Nicky asks.

"Fuckin' A!"

Anita listens to their conversation and says to Al, "Stop encouraging them to be criminals. They can get in a lot of trouble."

"I don't believe you assholes. Get rid of the damn thing and forget about makin' money. We're already in enough a shit," Stanzo says.

"Joo think it's goin' to take long? Joo crazy."

"Yeah, we can all get a share," Nicky says.

"Don't count me in on this," Stanzo says.

"Joo already in."

"Yeah well, I don't wanna be." Stanzo gives Ricky a look that could kill. Frankie looks at all of them and says, "Alright, if you guys want to strip it and sell the parts it's okay with me. Ya just gotta do it fast so we can dump it." Stanzo reacts with an I-can't-believe-you-guys look.

"Cool! I've already been talkin' to some people," Nicky says.

The girls have been listening to this conversation. Angela says, "Johnny Bonanno might be interested in somethin'. He's always buyin' car parts for those jalopies of his."

"We can talk to him," Ricky says.

Frankie downs his drink. "Good. Let's get rid of it this week."

A few more days go by. This early in the evening, only Ricky and Nicky sit at the bar next to a strange looking character. Al straightens things and cleans up behind the bar.

Johnny Bonanno, the Italian-American equivalent of poor white trash, has black greasy hands with a layer of crud under his fingernails. "I can give ya 300 for the engine and tranie," Johnny says.

Johnny smiles as he uses the back of his hand to wipe snot dripping from his unusually large nose. Ricky watches uncomfortably, and then takes a sip of beer to steady his stomach. "Three-hundred! Joo gotta be kiddin'."

"They're worth at least 300 each," Nicky says.

Johnny eyes bulge in disbelief. "Yeah? That's a lot."

"They're brand new. Only 8000 miles," Nicky says.

"Eight-thousand only? Where'd ya get this engine and tranie?"

"We just got them. That's all. Joo interested or not?"

Johnny wipes his nose again on his sleeve. "Yeah. I want 'em. But I only got 300. Maybe I can get another hundred."

Nicky tells him, "It ain't enough."

"Give me a few days, maybe I can get some more money."

"We'll try to hang onto them until joo come up with the money."

Nicky interjects, "We can't promise anything. A lot of people want them."

"Yeah?"

CHAPTER 15

Frankie's car and several other cars park on lovers' lane. Heavy breathing comes from inside the car while the soft doo-wop sounds of "You Belong to Me" plays on the radio. The glow from the radio reflects on Frankie and Gloria having sex in the back seat. Gloria has her skirt up around her waist, revealing her shapely thighs, and her legs wrap around Frankie's lower back. Frankie, his pants down around his ankles, pumps his manhood. Each thrust evokes a little squeal from Gloria and her breasts bounce. In a flurry of quick thrusts, a breathless Frankie finishes. Gloria's cheeks have a rosy red color.

Frankie removes himself from on top of Gloria. They both sit up and straighten their clothes. They look spent. Frankie lights a cigarette. "So when we gonna set the date so we don't have to do it in the car anymore?"

Gloria doesn't answer. She fixes her hair, pulls on her panties, puts on her bra and blouse, and lowers her skirt. She searches on the floor for her shoes, and puts them on. Frankie asks again, "So when ya wanna get married?"

She sits back against the seat. "I don't know. When do you want to do it?"

Frankie asks, "May?"

"May? That's too soon to plan a nice wedding. I want a big wedding. I have to find a dress, bridesmaids' dresses, and a place. That's a lot to do by May, Frankie."

Frankie offers, "We can have it at the restaurant." Gloria makes a disapproving face.

"What? We've had a lot of weddings there. We even have a great band, The Top Hats. They play everything from rock and roll to Italian songs."

"No! Not your restaurant."

Frankie fills with disappointment, and out of frustration asks, "What about June?"

"I don't know. June is still too soon. I'll have to talk to my parents."

"Well, can we decide soon?"

"What are you being so pushy about?"

"Because when ya give someone an engagement ring, you're supposed to pick a date for the wedding."

"People don't always do it right away."

Frankie sighs and his frustration rises close to anger. "I don't know—sometimes I think you can care less if ya marry me."

"Ah, come on Frankie. I love ya. Ya know that—and I want to marry you." She leans over and kisses his cheek. "Let's not argue about it."

"Fine." Frankie leans over, and kisses her on the lips, and they immediately embrace tightly.

The following night, lights go out in Russo's Restaurant. Frankie and his father come out the front door. Frankie locks the door, pulls the protective gate across the front of the restaurant, and locks it with a

98

padlock. They walk to the car and get in. Frankie starts the car and pulls away from the curb. "So, have you and Gloria decided on a date yet?" Albert asks.

"Nah, she still doesn't know when she wants to do it."

"Maybe it's best ya wait. You're both still young."

"I'm ready to get married Pop. If we wait too long, I might get my draft notice."

"Hey, don't worry. I spoke to Tony Limata. He says he might be able to pull some strings." Albert gives his son a wink of assurance.

"Yeah? I still want to get married. Ya want some more grandkids, don't ya?"

Frankie's brother has a girl five and a boy four; his sister has a nine-year-old boy, and two girls, one six and a two-year-old.

Smiling at the thought of more children in the family, Albert says, "That would be nice. Who knows how much longer I'll be around."

"Don't say that Pop. You're gonna be around a long time.

"God willing."

CHAPTER 16

Al watches the evening news on TV. Ricky and Nicky sit at the end of the bar. The TV newscaster says, "Two U.S. Navy jets flying low-altitude target reconnaissance over Laos were shot down today by Pathet Lao ground fire."

Nicky watches Ricky counting money. "Three-hundred-fifty-six," Ricky says.

"Ya sure?"

"Yeah."

Al comes over to them shaking his head. "Hey, put that away. Don't go flashin' all that money 'round here. Ya did good."

"Yeah, if Bonanno comes up with the dough, the engine and tranie are gone."

"He ain't comin' up with it. He's full'a shit. I got some other peoples I'm talkin' to," Ricky says.

"You guys better get rid of that thing pretty soon."

Stanzo walks in with Priscilla at his side. Everyone exchanges greetings. Ricky counts out some bills under the edge of the bar, folds them, and extends them towards Stanzo. Stanzo looks at the money. "What's this?"

"It's joor share... From the car... we sold the wheels and tires and Frankie's old radio."

"I told ya. I don't want it."

Priscilla leans into him and says, "You should take it. It looks like a lot of money. You can use it for that car you want to buy."

"Don't you start with me. I don't want it."

"Fuck it. We'll split it between us," Nicky says.

"Al, give me a Schaefer and a coke for my girl," Stanzo says.

"Gotcha..."

"Al, can I have two cherries."

"Ya sure can, doll."

Al serves them their drinks. "Can we sit in a booth?" Priscilla asks.

"Sure," Stanzo says and looks behind him at the empty booths. He and Priscilla get up and go sit down; Nicky and Ricky join them. They all look up as Frankie walks through the front door. He stops at the booth and says, "We gotta get rid of it."

"As soon as we get rid of the engine and tranie, we start cuttin' it up. I got my old man's torch as soon as we're ready," Nicky says.

"So what about Bonanno?"

"He can't get the 600," Ricky says.

"Did it ever occur to ya that 600 is too much? It's stolen property. Ya ain't gonna get retail pricing," Stanzo says.

"That asshole don't even have three," Nicky says.

Frankie says, "Al, give me a seven and seven." He looks at the others. "Anybody need a drink?" They all shake their heads no. Frankie picks up his drink and sits in the booth.

"Why don't ya just take the 300 and get rid of it?" Stanzo asks.

"Joo kidding? It's cheap. It's worth 600 easy. Its only got 8000 miles."

"You're fuckin' crazy," Stanzo says.

Raising his voice, Nicky says to Stanzo, "Fuck you!"

"Yeah? Fuck you!" Stanzo says.

"Hey, watch your language," Priscilla says.

Stanzo gets up and pulls Priscilla along with him. Ricky grabs Stanzo's arm and says, "Come on man..."

Stanzo glares at Ricky and pulls his arm away as Hanna walks through the front door and sits down in her usual spot at the bar. Stanzo glares at Ricky and says, "Fuck you."

"Fuck joo!"

As the argument gets louder than the music playing on the jukebox Frankie interjects, trying to keep the peace, "Hey, come on. We'll... we'll just get rid of it."

Al leans over the bar, points a finger at Stanzo. "Hey, I got customers here. Let's keep it down or take it outside." Stanzo glares at Al. He's about to say something, then grabs Priscilla's arm and pulls her towards the door. Stanzo is about to walk out when he turns to his friends, points to Ricky and says, "Fuck you!" Then to Nicky, "Fuck you!"

From her seat at the bar, Hanna says, "Hey! Watch your language over there."

Al says, "Hey, Stanzo, what did I just tell ya?"

Stanzo turns to Al and looks about to curse Al out but decides otherwise. Instead, he pulls Priscilla by the arm. She stumbles out the door behind him. The others stare after them.

"Hey, take it easy! Ya shouldn't fight with your friends," Priscilla says.

They walk down the street. "They're greedy assholes and they're gonna get busted."

Back in the bar, Al leans on the bar top and tells the guys, "Let's get somethin' straight here. He's your friend. Ya don't treat a friend like that. What the hell's wrong with you guys?"

"He started it," Nicky says.

"He thinks he knows everythin'," Ricky adds.

Al looks at them and shakes his head in disbelief. "He happens to be right. You guys don't watch your asses you're gonna be in jail. Don't get greedy. Ya get rid of it as soon as you can. I told ya that from the start. You're dealin' with hot merchandise. Ya start talkin' to a lot of people—you're gonna get fucked up." Al looks at them for a long moment to get his point across.

"Yeah, you're right Al. I'll call him tomorrow and apologize," Frankie says.

Satisfied, Al nods and walks away.

"Yeah, thanks Al," Frankie says.

CHAPTER 17

Another Saturday night at Al's, Ricky sits with the girls at the far end of the bar near the pool table. Behind them, Charlie and Nicky shoot a game of pool.

Maryanne has a little more eye makeup on tonight and wears a low cut blouse that reveals a lot more cleavage than normal. It gives her a rather seductive, attractive look. She says, "Benny's with her every night."

Charlie walks over to Maryanne with his usual mischievous smile as he gazes down at her cleavage. "Yeah, well I would be too."

"Charlie you'd do it to a rug if it had a pussy," Pinkie says.

They all laugh at Charlie's expense. "Oh, yeah?"

The front door opens and Frankie and Gloria walk in. Gloria has on a short black skirt and tight white sweater. The guys almost drool when they see her. The girls have a completely different reaction as their faces reflect their dislike for Gloria. "Hi, everybody," Frankie says.

"Hi!" Gloria offers cheerfully.

"Oh, hi Gloria." Angela says.

Frankie and Gloria sit on the open barstools next to Ricky. Al walks over to them. "What can I get ya?"

"A whiskey sour on the rocks for Gloria. I'll have a seven and seven, Al." Frankie looks at the others. "Can I get anyone else something?"

Pinkie pipes in, "Yeah, we'll take another round." Frankie nods an okay to Al. Nicky says, "Al, I'll take another beer."

Al pours drinks and puts them in front of everyone. "Stanzo been in?" Frankie asks Al.

"Nah. I haven't seen him. He's probably still pissed at you assholes. Ya know he's got a telephone. Ya could call him."

"Al, I did. His mother said she'd tell him I called."

"Like I said, he's probably still pissed." Al walks over to the cash register and puts Frankie's money in.

"He's in love," Angela says.

Pinkie says, "That's right."

Almost in tears, Maryanne says, "Don't say that. He's not in love—with her." She looks at Pinkie and says, "I don't know why you had to bring her around here."

"I'm sorry. I didn't know this was gonna happen," Pinkie pleads.

"Charlie comes over to Maryanne and puts his arm around her. "What's a matter, Maryanne? Come on I'll take ya for a ride"

"Thanks Charl, but no thanks."

Charlie says defensively, "I'd rather drink beer."

"Fuck you Ferraro," Pinkie says.

"I heard she's married?" Maryanne says.

"Married?" Charlie asks.

"Yeah, that's what we heard Charl," Pinkie says.

"Stanzo know?" Charlie asks.

"I don't think so. And don't be the big mouth who tells him," Maryanne says.

"Not me. Who's she married to?"

"We heard some sailor," Angela says.

Gloria leans forward and asks, "Who are you talking about."

"Some Spanish girl that Pinkie brought here," Maryanne says.

"Oh."

Ricky says to Frankie, "Joo was to the garage?"

"Yeah. I couldn't believe it. You guys have been busy. I'm gonna have to get wheels to put on it."

"We got money for joo."

"I don't want it. Ya split it between ya."

"Yeah? Joo don't want it? Joo can use it to get tires."

"No." Frankie whispers, "We gotta get rid of that thing."

Gloria's ears perk up. "What are you talking about? she asks.

"Oh, just some old car the guys have been taking apart," Frankie says. The girls smile at each other, knowing that Frankie's afraid to tell Gloria the truth.

Ricky tells Frankie, "We got a guy who's gonna let us know about the engine and tranie this week."

"What happened to Bonanno?"

Nicky says, "He ain't got no money."

"If that guy doesn't want them—that's it. We dump it."

"Alright," Ricky says.

Gloria laces her arm in Frankie's and whispers something in his ear. "Hey, we came by to see if ya wanna go out to the Yellow Brick Road. Gloria wants to go dancin'."

"Yeah, we wanna go," Pinkie, says.

The others all agree that they want to go. They finish their drinks and pick their money off the bar. Frankie gets up. "See ya later Al."

"Yeah."

They all leave the bar. Al watches them as they walk out.

A couple of hours later, Anita sits at the bar talking with Al. "Honey, if it doesn't get any busier, why don't ya close early? she says.

"Yeah, I might do that."

Al notices three cars pulling up in front of the bar. The door opens and JoJo and twelve of his boys walk in. They scan the bar suspiciously. Al senses trouble. JoJo smiles at Anita; she returns the smile. "What's up JoJo?" Al asks.

"How ya doin' Al?"

"Good. Business is good."

"Yeah? It don't' look so good. Looks like a morgue in here." JoJo's buddies laugh.

"Yeah, well it's still early. What can I get ya?

"Nothin'. We're not stayin'."

Jokingly, Al says, "Should I be grateful?"

JoJo doesn't get the humor. "Whatta ya mean?"

"Nothin'. Just joking."

"That Stanzo been in?"

Al busily wipes down the bar top. "Haven't seen him."

JoJo gazes around the bar. He nods to his boys to look in the back. Two of them walk into the back room and even look in the restrooms. They come out shaking their heads.

"When ya see him, tell 'im I wanna talk to 'im."

"Whatta ya wanna talk to him about?"

"Somebody smacked my uncle in the head last night on his way home from Mikey's."

"So what's that got to do with Stanzo?"

JoJo appears annoyed with the question. "My uncle's his ex-girlfriend's old man."

"Linda?"

"Yeah, Linda."

"So he says it was Stanzo?"

"Nah, he don't know for sure. But he thinks it was Stanzo."

"So ya don't know it was Stanzo."

"I know it was him."

"Now, what would he do somthin' like that for?"

"'Cause he's a wise ass and he ain't too bright."

"Um..." Al says sarcastically, "Well, that makes sense. If I see him I'll tell him ya were in."

JoJo's boys return to the front.

"Thanks." To his thugs he says, "Let's go!" And to Al he says, "Hope business gets better."

"Yeah, me too."

Al's revulsion shows as he watches them leave. Anita says, "They're looking for trouble."

"Yeah, I know. Stanzo better watch out."

CHAPTER 18

Stanzo lives in a white-shingled, two-story house on Roosevelt Avenue under the El, only a block away from Al's bar. In Stanzo's dark bedroom, he and Priscilla's naked bodies writhe on the bed. The squeaking bedsprings compete with heavy breathing and the rumble of the occasional train outside his window. The breathing gets louder and louder and builds to a crescendo. The body movements slow down and eventually stop. Stanzo rolls off Priscilla and tries to breathe normally again. Priscilla lays her head on his chest.

Stanzo reaches down to his crotch and feels around. "Oh fuck! Shit! Fuck, fuck, fuck."

"What? What! What's the matter?"

"The rubber broke."

"Don't worry. I never get pregnant."

"Whatta ya mean?"

Priscilla lifts her head and looks down at him. "I never get pregnant."

"How many times have you done it? No, never mind. I don't want to hear it." He sits up.

"You're mad at me?"

"I ain't mad. I just... it's just that I don't like that you've been with other guys."

"Oh, and what about you? You've had a lot of girlfriends."

"That's different—I'm a guy."

Priscilla finds great pleasure in mimicking Stanzo. "That's different—I'm a guy."

"Hey don't fuck with me."

Priscilla giggles and mimics. "Hey don't fuck with me."

Priscilla throws her arms around him and locks him in another passionate embrace until Stanzo suddenly breaks away. He looks over at the clock on his night table. "Hey, we gotta get out of here. My mother and father are gonna be home soon."

"You don't want to do it again?"

"Yeah, I do, but not now. Come on." He jumps out of bed and starts dressing. Priscilla does too.

Back at Al's, the door pops open and Frankie, the guys and girls enter, much to Al's surprise. They take seats at the bar. Al asks, "What are ya doin' back already?"

"The band didn't show up and the place was empty," Frankie says.

Anita looks at Al with a hopeless expression, until Al finally says, "JoJo and his assholes were in here. They're looking for Stanzo."

"No shit," Frankie says.

Nicky asks, "Whatta they want?"

"Trouble. Somebody better tell Stanzo."

JoJo's car cruises the streets of Corona. He and three of his thugs look out the windows for Stanzo.

Stanzo and Priscilla come out of his house and walk down the street. Stanzo, sensing uneasiness, looks over his shoulder. "What's the matter?" Priscilla asks.

"Nothin'."

They don't notice JoJo's car turning the corner and slowly coming towards them. Inside the car, one of JoJo's boys points down the street. JoJo steps on the gas and the car accelerates towards Stanzo and Priscilla. The car comes to a screeching stop. Stanzo and Priscilla turn in the direction of squealing tires as JoJo and company jump out of the car and surround them.

JoJo throws a punch, catching Stanzo on the chin. Priscilla screams. Stanzo quickly swings back and hits JoJo in the stomach. JoJo doubles over, but his boys jump on Stanzo. Priscilla tries to pull them off and throws punches; they push her aside until one of the guys grabs her around the waist. She kicks backwards catching him in the shin. She scratches his bare arms, and bites his bicep. He pushes her away and she crashes to the ground. JoJo and the other two guys pummel Stanzo. Priscilla gets up and instead of helping her boyfriend, she runs away.

Uncertain about where to go, she finds herself at the corner across from Al's Bar & Grill. Priscilla runs across the street and through the front door. Her face lights as she sees Stanzo's friends sitting at the bar and she screams. "Help! Help!"

Everyone turns to her. "They're beating him up!"

Nicky grabs Priscilla's arm and asks, "Who?"

"That JoJo and his friends. Down the block..."

Nicky and her rush out the door. Some of the guys grab beer bottles and follow. Al pulls a baseball bat out from under the bar. "Watch the bar," he says to Anita. He climbs over the bar and follows them out the door.

By the time his friends arrive, they find Stanzo crunching in a protective ball on the sidewalk. JoJo and his boys pound and kick him. JoJo looks up and notices Frankie and the guys coming in their direction. They turn away from Stanzo and head for the car. Stanzo tries to get up and collapses to the ground. Priscilla runs over to comfort him.

JoJo and his gang don't get to their car fast enough. Nicky traps JoJo between the open car door and the car frame, pinning his arms at his side. "Get the fuck outta here, Vitalli!" JoJo says. Nicky puts all his body weight against the door and throws punches at JoJo's head.

Frankie charges into two of JoJo's boys, knocking them to the ground. Charlie and Ricky break their beer bottles on two guys' heads. JoJo struggles to free himself. Nicky unleashes punch after punch at JoJo's face, blood spurts from his nose. In between Nicky's punches, Jo Jo glances in horror as Al raises his bat above the car's windshield. "Not my fuckin' car! You son-of-a-bitch."

Al smashes the bat into the windshield, while Ricky pierces the car tires with his broken bottle. Nicky continues to punch JoJo into oblivion. Obviously, Frankie and his friends have gotten the best of these guys.

A little while later, back in the bar, Stanzo sits with his head slightly forward. Anita gently applies a towel with ice to his swollen and sore face. Al places a shot glass of whiskey in front of Stanzo. "Here drink this." Stanzo picks up the glass and downs the whiskey.

"Thanks Al." Al nods.

Anita hands the towel to Priscilla sitting on the other side of Stanzo. He winces when Priscilla places the ice against his face. Stanzo tries to remove it. "Leave it! It'll keep the swelling down," Anita says.

"It fuckin' hurts!" His friends watch and feel for him.

"I know. Just keep it there."

"Linda's father's whole head is bandaged," Pinkie says.

Stanzo turns to her, looking innocent and says, "Hey, I didn't do that. The prick probably fell. He's always loaded."

"JoJo's gotta be hurtin' too. I heard ribs crack when I slammed the door on him," Nicky says.

Maryanne looks compassionately at Stanzo and says, "Benny, you should go home and rest."

"I'm alright."

"Well you don't look so good." Maryanne looks from him to Priscilla.

"She's right. You should go home," Priscilla agrees.

Frankie says, "Come on. I'll drive ya."

"Ya better get some rest," Al says.

Stanzo's friends help him to his feet. He hands the towel to Al. "Nah, you take it with ya," Al says.

Stanzo looks gratefully at his friends, "Hey, thanks. I missed you assholes."

Everyone watches as Priscilla and Frankie on either side of Stanzo make their way slowly to the door. Gloria follows them out the door.

CHAPTER 19

Several weeks have gone by since they beat up JoJo and his boys. Surprisingly, there haven't been any repercussions, but Frankie and his friend have been on guard. The stolen car still sits in Frankie's garage gathering dust.

The guys minus the girls sit at the bar. Stanzo shows no signs of the beating he took. Al busily dries glasses. The door opens and Frankie walks in. He doesn't look terribly happy. He pulls up a stool. "Let me have a seven and seven, Al."

"What's a matter? Had a fight with your girlfriend?" Al teases.

Frankie removes a letter from his pocket with a subway token stuck to it. "Look what I got."

"Oh, shit man. I'm sorry," Al says. It catches everyone's attention.

Charlie comes up behind Frankie and puts his hand on Frankie's shoulder. "When did ya get it?"

"Yesterday."

"When joo gotta go?" Ricky asks.

"Three weeks."

"That's a bitch. Hey, man. I might sign up," Nicky says.

They all look at him in disbelief. "Joo ain't goin' nowhere," Ricky says.

Nicky says, "I might." They don't take him seriously and turn their attention back to Frankie.

"My old man's tryin' to pull some strings to get me reclassified. I ain't countin' on it, though. Listen, we gotta get rid of that thing tonight," Frankie says.

"Tonight?" Ricky asks.

"Yeah, tonight. The landlord keeps asking me about it. He keeps telling me he doesn't want junk in his garage. He sees you guys stripping it. I think he might be getting suspicious. And I don't want him to talk to my old man."

"How ya gonna drive it? There's no wheels, no seats, no dash..." Stanzo says.

"I picked up some wheels and tires at the junkyard and put them on today. I got a milk box to sit on," Frankie says.

"Oh, that's gonna be fun," Ricky says.

"I don't care. It's gotta go."

Stanzo shows a look of concern and says, "If we're gonna do it, we should do it around midnight. The cops change shifts then. You won't see them on the streets for at least a half hour."

Al says, "He's right. That's a good time to do it."

Nicky looks over at Frankie. "Where we gonna dump it?" he asks.

Al interjects, "Drive it to the other side of 37th Avenue. Just park it in the first place ya find. They'll think somebody around there dumped it. If nobody sees ya, they won't know how it got there."

Frankie tells them, "Alright, we go over there at eleven-thirty!"

"Who's gonna drive it?" Al asks.

Nicky responds, "Shit I'll drive it again."

"What are ya talkin' about—ya still don't have a license," Stanzo says.

"I'm gonna drive it. You guys have done enough," Frankie says.

Al reminds them, "Don't go through no lights or nothin'. No speeding, Frankie."

"That's gonna be hard to do, sitting on a milk box."

Frankie's car pulls into the driveway to his garage. The lights go out and the engine shuts off. Frankie, Stanzo, Nicky, and Ricky climb out of the car. Frankie opens the trunk and grabs a milk box. They walk towards the garage door. Frankie unlocks the door, pulls it open, finds the light switch, and turns on the lights; the guys follow him in.

The car doesn't look the same. It has a heavy coat of dust all over that previously shiny white exterior; it has no right fender and no bumper. The inside has no seats, and wires hang in-place of the missing dashboard. Frankie places the milk box for a driver's seat. He climbs in and sits on it. Nicky laughs and says, "Ya look like a little kid sittin' on that box."

Frankie ignores the comment as he sticks his key in the ignition, pumps the gas pedal, and turns the key. The engine laboriously groans and tries to start. Frankie tries it again. This time it barely cranks at all. "The battery's dead," Stanzo says.

Frankie, with disappointment written all over his face, looks at Stanzo. He tries it again. "Shit!" He tries once more. The silence frustrates Frankie further.

"It's dead," Nicky says as he walks around the front and lifts the hood. Frankie gets out of the car and they all join Nicky. Nicky removes one of the battery caps and sticks his finger into the battery. He does the same with another cap. "It's dried out. Ya ain't gonna get this started," he says.

"Joo got no cables?" Ricky asks.

Frankie shakes his head no. "Shit! I should'a tried starting it today."

While they look at each other and think about their next move, JoJo's car drives slowly down the street followed by two other cars. They stop in front of Frankie's driveway and notice his car. They pull over to the curb; the doors open on all three cars and JoJo and his boys step out.

In the garage, Nicky pulls down the hood. Frankie says, "I'll get a battery, and we'll get rid of it tomorrow night. Let's get out of here before the landlord sees us."

"Drop me off at Priscilla's!" Stanzo says.

Frankie looks at him needing an explanation. "Now?"

"Yeah, she sneaks me into her bedroom through the window."

They all look at him enviously. "Cool," Nicky says.

Frankie turns out the garage light, temporarily blinding them from seeing JoJo walking up the driveway carrying a baseball bat. Some of his boys have bats too. JoJo reaches the back of Frankie's car and swings the bat, smashing one of the taillights. One of his boys slams the other light. Glass and metal fragments fly everywhere.

The sound of bats slamming into the Bonneville startles Frankie and his friends. In the darkness, they barely make out the figures tearing through the convertible top and smashing the windshield.

Before they even recognize the intruders, Frankie and his friends charge towards them. Nicky tears into one of the guys, about to smash a headlight. JoJo continues bashing the car and inflicting new damage wherever he can. One of his other boys starts slashing Frankie's tires with a switchblade.

Frankie and his friends level into the enemy, despite the overwhelming odds against them. Each of them has at least two of JoJo's boys beating on them. JoJo seems in a trance as he feverishly finds new locations on the car to bash. His boys pound away at Frankie, Stanzo, Nicky, and Ricky.

In the commotion, no one notices lights coming on inside the house. The light over the back door flashes on. The landlord comes out wearing a robe and slippers, looks at the melee, lifts his shotgun into the air, and fires. The loud blast stops everyone. Lights come on in surrounding houses and a few windows open. The landlord levels his gun towards the melee. "Frankie! Is that you?"

In a shaky voice and with one guy holding him from behind and another one throwing punches at him, Frankie answers, "Yeah!"

"Are ya alright?"

"No!"

The two guys stop punching Frankie. JoJo notices the shotgun and asks, "Who's this crazy bastard?"

"He's my landlord."

They hear sirens approaching in the distance. JoJo shouts to the others, "Let's go! Let's get out of here." JoJo and his thugs scramble for their cars. They jump in and quickly pull away. They leave Frankie and his friends hurt with blood all over their torn clothes. Frankie's car looks even worse than they do.

A police cruiser with sirens wailing and red light flashing comes to stop in front of the driveway. "Oh, shit," Frankie says. Two police officers get out and walk towards Frankie's car.

The landlord with his shotgun at his side stands with the boys, appraising the damage to the car. One of the cops, a young guy not much older than Frankie and his friends has a handsome face and tall, muscular body. The other guy, an older looking cop in his late thirties, has a stomach that hangs over his belt. He looks at the landlord and asks, "What're ya doin' with that shotgun, sir?"

"Protectin' my property, officer."

The older policemen asks, "You the one fired it?"

"Yeah, these boys were getting' beat up."

"Who was beating you up?" the older cop asks.

Frankie quickly answers, "We don't know who they are."

"You don't, hah?"

"We've never seen them before."

The cop takes the gun and smells the barrel. The younger cop examines the damage to Frankie's car. "This car yours?" he asks the landlord.

"Nah, it's his," pointing to Frankie.

"What happened here?" the older cop asks.

"I told ya. These guys were beatin' them up. Sep't it looks like his car got the worst of it." He laughs. The policemen don't find it amusing.

"You're sure you don't know who these guys were?" the younger cop asks.

Frankie and his friends shrug their shoulders and look away. Frankie looks uncomfortably towards the still open garage door. The younger cop notices the other car and asks, "Whose car is that?"

"That's his, too." The landlord points to Frankie, "He had an accident and fixed his car with the parts from that one," the landlord says.

"Oh, yeah?" the younger cop asks. He walks towards the garage. In the semi-darkness, Frankie's face turns ashen. He avoids looking at his friends who fidget nervously. The older cop watches as the garage light comes on. The police officer pokes his head inside the car, walks around it, and opens the driver's side door. He takes out his flashlight and shines it inside the car. He opens the hood, flashes his light on the engine, takes out a book and pen, and writes down the VIN number. The older cop glances at the garage, then back at Frankie. "Where'd ya say ya got that car?" he asks.

Before Frankie thinks of what to say the landlord answers, "He got it from his friend who got drafted."

The older cop throws the landlord a disparaging look. The younger one comes back and says to Frankie, "Let me see your license and the registration for both of these cars!"

Frankie responds, "You know Captain Kelly?"

The young police officer says, "No. I ain't gonna ask you again. Your license and registration!"

Frankie removes his wallet from his pocket and hands over his license and registration. "I don't have the one for the other car on me. Sergeant Halliday at the 119th is a good friend of mine."

The cop looking over Frankie's paperwork doesn't say anything. Frankie tries again, "Hey, ya know Captain Kennedy?"

The older cop looks at him curiously, probably wondering how Frankie knows all these police officers. "Captain Kennedy? Yeah. He's a nice guy."

"He's a good friend of mine, too," Frankie says optimistically.

"That's good," the older cop says.

"I'm gonna radio in this VIN," the younger cop says.

The other cop watches Frankie's face flush as the young cop walks toward the cruiser, gets in, and picks up the radio mike. Frankie's friends shift nervously. Stanzo throws Frankie an I-told-you-so look.

CHAPTER 20

On the way to the police station, Frankie sits in the back of the police car by himself, thinking, *why did I do such a stupid thing*? They put his friends in another police car arriving at the fight scene shortly after the first two cops.

Later in an interrogation room, Detective Colucci grills Frankie. The detective who's in his mid-thirties wears an ill-fitting black suit and a tie with red and blue strips. He has receding red hair and freckles. Colucci takes notes on a yellow legal pad. Frankie looks worn out. Colucci asks, "What about your buddies? Did they help you steal the car?"

Frankie, not wanting to implicate his friends, says, "They didn't have anything to do with it." But he wonders about his friends, and hopes they keep their mouths shut.

"You're sure they didn't have anything to do with it?

"Yeah, I'm sure."

"You're saying they didn't help you in any way?"

Frankie nods in agreement.

"They knew you had an accident?"

"Yeah but they weren't around that night."

"Ya sure they weren't around? Your landlord says two other guys helped ya."

"I told ya. They didn't have anything to do with it."

"Come on I know they helped you."

More vehemently, Frankie tells him again, "They had nothin' to do with it!"

Colucci looks down at his pad. He searches for something in his mind, perhaps a new tack. "So if your car was wrecked, how'd you find the other car?"

Frankie hesitates to answer, then says, "I borrowed someone's car."

"Whose car?"

"A friend."

"What's your friend's name?"

"I ain't gonna tell ya that."

"It's just for the record. It's no big deal."

Frankie stares at the cop through weary eyes.

"Your friend isn't in any trouble. The sooner you give us his name, the faster we can get out of here. You wanna go home don't you? So what's his name?"

"You're sure it's just for the record?"

Frankie in a tired voice says, "Charlie... Charlie Ferraro." And as soon as he says it, he wishes he hadn't.

In the police station lobby, Stanzo, Nicky, and Ricky half sit on a wooden bench opposite the front desk. The police suspect their involvement in the theft, but without a confession or a positive I.D. from the landlord, they have nothing to charge them with.

A beefy sergeant sits at a high desk overseeing the comings and goings in the station. "Shit man, we're going to jail. I know it. I just know it," Ricky whispers to his friends.

"He ain't gonna rat on us," Nicky says.

"He ain't? They ask joo lots of tricky questions when they have joo in there."

"They asked me 'bout the night in the park. When we broke into the park office," Ricky says.

"I forgot about that. They asked me, too" Stanzo says.

"They gonna get us in there again. Joo watch."

The phone ringing at the front desk distracts them. They watch the desk sergeant pick it up. He looks over at the guys while he listens. "I'll tell them." He hangs up the phone. "Hey! You guys. Over here!"

Stanzo, Nicky, and Ricky get up and walk slowly, as if on a death march. "Ya friend's gonna be stayin' a while. Ya can go home. We got your information if we need ya. Ya need a ride home?" the sergeant asks.

Stanzo quickly answers, "Nah, we can walk home."

"Awright, you're free to go."

The guys can't believe their ears and quickly exit the station house.

Nicky, Ricky, and Stanzo head to Al's first thing. They feel safe inside the dimly lit bar as they watch Al clean up in anticipation of closing. The guys down strong drinks. "They wouldn't have let ya go if they thought ya were involved," Al says.

"My old man'll kick my ass if I get arrested. He always says, 'Ya get in trouble with the cops ya gonna rot in jail before I come to get ya,'" Nicky says.

"Listen, he didn't rat you guys out."

"Yeah, well Frankie would never do that," Stanzo says.

"I hope you're right. I ain't goin' home tonight, If they come to my house, I ain't gonna be there." Nicky says.

In the wee hours of the morning, back at the police station, the young cop from earlier approaches the front desk with a weary looking Charlie. He says to the desk sergeant, "See if you got a rap sheet on a Charles Ferraro. He's under arrest for grand larceny."

The color drains from Charlie's face. "What? I thought ya said ya just wanted to ask me some questions."

The police officer turns to him and says, "Ya buddy Frank Russo implicated you in the theft of a 1964 Pontiac Bonneville."

Charlie gets a grim look on his face and decides to keep his mouth shut. The desk sergeant asks, "What's your address son?"

"104-68 41st Avenue."

The sergeant hands a piece of paper to the other officer who looks it over, turns to Charlie, and says, "Breaking and entering Linden Park custodian's office in 1959. Charges dropped. Ya ain't gonna be so lucky this time, Charlie."

CHAPTER 21

Frankie, his father, and their attorney, Tony Limata, a short man with gray hair wearing thick glasses with black frames, walk out of the Queens County Courthouse after posting bail. Frankie looks in desperate need of sleep. No one says anything as they walk to Tony's Cadillac. Albert gets in the front seat of the car and Frankie gets in the back. Albert doesn't look well; worry creases his face. When Tony gets in the car and starts it, Albert asks, "What do you think?"

"Well if he pleads guilty—he has a clean record—they'll probably go easy on him."

Frankie listens from the back seat but doesn't say anything.

Later the same day, Frankie enters the kitchen after some rest, a shower, and clean clothes. His father looks up briefly from his newspaper and drinks from a cup of coffee. Frankie asks, "Any coffee left?"

"In the pot."

Frankie feels his father's icy demeanor and wants to say something comforting, but finds it difficult as he grabs an empty cup from the cabinet and pours coffee. He looks over at his father as he goes to the refrigerator and adds milk. He puts the milk back, and scoops two teaspoons of sugar into his cup and stirs. Frankie pulls out a chair and sits across from his dad.

Albert looks at his son and says, "Uncle Ralph is picking me up at three o'clock for work. You don't have to come in tonight. Stay home and rest."

"Ya sure. 'Cause I feel better."

More vehemently, he says, "You stay home and rest!"

Frankie feeling his father's anger, says, "Dad, I'm sorry. It was a stupid thing I did. I know it now. I don't know what I was thinking."

"You know what hurts Frankie?"

Unable to answer, Frankie shakes his head.

"The way you lied to me."

Frankie feels terrible and covers his eyes with his hand, and bows his head in resignation.

"Telling me you got the seats and everything from a friend. I had no reason not to believe you. You never lied to me like that before. I always trusted you, son. You've always been a good boy."

A long silence follows. Frankie removes his hand from over his eyes. "I know Pop."

Albert looks at him as though hoping for more. "When the police called last night, I thought I was having a bad dream. He told me three times before it sunk in that they arrested you. 'You sure it's my son Frankie?' I had to ask." He looks at Frankie with moist eyes.

"I didn't want to tell you I had another accident, but this is even worse."

Albert raises his voice uncharacteristically, "What the hell were you thinking?"

"I don't know. I was feeling terrible about the car; Gloria disappointed me about getting married... I guess I wasn't myself... I wasn't thinking clearly. I didn't want to go steal the car, but it all seemed so easy. I didn't think this would happen."

"This is one time that I'm glad your mother's not around. She would be very upset with you. She loved you very much. No one in our family has ever been arrested before."

"I'm sorry, Pop." Albert looks back at his paper. Frankie doesn't know what else to say. He gets up, takes his coffee cup with him, and walks out of the room.

That night at Al's, Stanzo, Nicky, and Ricky sit at the bar. Al asks, "You guys talk to Frankie? They shake their heads no. "I don't know about Charlie not rattin' on ya."

"Charlie ain't gonna rat. He'll fuck your girlfriend but he won't rat on ya," Stanzo says.

"Speaking of girlfriends, how come you're not with Priscilla?" Nicky asks.

"She's been actin' weird lately."

"I feel bad for Charlie. He didn't want to lend us his car anyway. You guys badgered him into it," Stanzo says. Nicky and Ricky have guilty looks on their faces. "The one I'm worried about is the landlord. He knows our faces," Nicky says.

"Yeah, well there's nothin' ya can do about it now," Al says. A serious look comes over Al's face as he gazes out the front window. The guys turn their attention to what Al sees—a police car cruising slowly past the bar. To their relief, the car keeps going.

CHAPTER 22

News about the stolen car, and the arrests of the two guys, has the whole neighborhood abuzz. The local newspaper provides enough information about the robbery to fuel the rumor mill. Frankie, Stanzo, Ricky, and Nicky sit at Al's bar. They feel anxious, waiting for the other shoe to drop. Frankie says, "I didn't say anything about you guys. As far as they know, I did this all by myself."

"Yeah, easy for you to say," Stanzo says. "What about the guy who owns the garage?"

"He already told the cops he didn't recognize anybody."

Nicky says, "My old man was asking me if I knew anything about it."

"We don't know what Charlie told them," Stanzo says.

They all turn as the door opens, and who walks in but Charlie. He stands in the doorway, his face red as he glares at Frankie. "Charlie!" Frankie says.

Charlie doesn't answer. Al shouts, "Hey, close the door!" Charlie closes the door behind him.

Frankie jumps off his stool and turns to Charlie. "Charlie, I'm sorry."

Frankie doesn't know how to react as Charlie just stares at him. "I didn't tell them anything about you... honest," Frankie says.

Charlie moves aggressively towards Frankie. He opens his arms and says, "I know. The fuckers tricked you into giving them my name."

"How'd ya know?"

Charlie puts his arms around Frankie. "The young cop told me."

The other guys watch the two of them embracing. Charlie asks, "Ya ready for court tomorrow?"

They separate. "Yeah." Frankie turns around and says, "Al, see what he wants to drink."

"I'll take a Schaefer."

Charlie sits next to Frankie at the bar. Frankie says, "Hey, I don't have to worry about the draft for awhile. Limata says they won't take me if I plead guilty. He's gonna try to get me a suspended sentence with no jail time."

"That's good."

Charlie looks at the other guys. "I didn't tell them nothin' about you assholes."

"See, I told ya not to worry about Charlie," Al says.

The courthouse, a large white marble building with steep steps leads to glass front doors. Inside the courtroom, Frankie stands at the defense table next to his attorney. Charlie stands next to Frankie. Charlie's attorney, Louie D'Leo, an elderly, overweight man in a wrinkly black mohair suit, stands at his side.

Frankie's father sits behind them. Charlie's mother, a petite woman in her fifties with graying hair, wears a navy blue dress and sits next to Albert. On the bench, an elderly, stern-looking judge with spectacles looks down at the defendants. His nameplate reads "Judge Clayton."

Sitting in the rear of the room, a young, attractive blonde about the same age as Frankie and Charlie watches the proceedings with interest. "In the case of the people versus Charles Ferraro, how do you plead?" the judge asks.

Charlie answers, "Not guilty."

"In the case of the people versus Frank Russo, how do you plead?"

"Guilty," Frankie says.

Tony Limata says, "Your honor, my client has completely cooperated with the investigation and has no previous record. I'd like that to be reflected in the record."

"It is so noted and will be taken into consideration during the sentencing phase. In the case of people versus Charles Ferraro, trial date is set for November 14th. In the case of people versus Frank Russo, sentencing is scheduled for November 9th. Next case," the judge says, banging his gavel.

Frankie, Charlie, and their parents walk out the front door of the courthouse. As they start down the steps, the blonde from court rushes up to Frankie and blocks his path. An uncertain Frankie looks at the beautiful girl and wonders what she wants. Frankie stares into her light blue eyes; short blond hair encircles her face with its puffy pink checks and freckles. She wears an expensive-looking black overcoat open in the front. Frankie glances at her full breasts and shapely body.

She stares at Frankie scornfully and says, "That was my car you stole. You have some balls!"

When she hears the word "balls," Charlie's mother blushes and closes her eyes.

Frankie attempts a smile, trying to lighten the situation, but the blonde turns away and walks down the steps.

Later that night, Frankie and Gloria sit on her living room couch. You can cut the tension between them as Gloria fidgets with her engagement ring, twisting it this way and that on her finger. "My parents don't want me engaged to someone in jail."

Frankie pleads, "I'm not in jail."

"But you're going to one, Frankie. You stole a car."

"I know but my lawyer says I probably won't have to go to jail.

"No? Well I hope he's right."

"This is silly. I love you. I wanna marry you."

Gloria looks on the verge of tears. "My parents don't want me marrying a criminal."

"I'm not a criminal."

"What'd you have to steal a car for?" Gloria dabs at her eyes with a tissue, and the tears make Frankie feel bad.

"I don't know why I did it. I just did. It was stupid." Trying to change the subject, Frankie says,

"Hey, I probably won't have to go in the army now. Ya didn't want me to go... did ya?"

"I didn't, but I didn't think you were gonna go out and steal a car to get out of it." She removes the engagement ring and hands it to Frankie. "You should go."

"What's this?"

"I'm breaking off our engagement."

"Oh, come on Gloria," Frankie pleads.

"Ya better go. My parents are gonna be home soon. I don't want you to be here when they do. My father's very angry with you."

"Well maybe I can talk to them."

Gloria shakes her head no.

Frankie reaches out for her but she pushes his hand away. He senses the futility of the situation, gets up, and reluctantly leaves.

Stanzo has his own female problems with Priscilla. He and Priscilla walk down the street, and he watches as the streetlights illuminate her pretty face. She feels distant to him. "Why do you have to go home so early?"

"I just have to—and stop asking me why, why, why. I just do, damn it."

"Then I'll come over later."

"No, you can't."

"You've been actin' strange all week. Whatta ya havin' your period?"

Priscilla stops walking and glares at him with contempt. "No—I'm not having my period. You really want to know what's bothering me. I'll tell you. For your information, I'm not gonna have my period because I'm pregnant."

Stanzo's face turns white. "What? I thought ya said ya never get pregnant."

"I never did before."

"Ya sure?"

"Yeah, I'm sure."

They start walking again. Stanzo hangs his head "Oh shit. I can't believe this. I told you to let me use those rubbers. Whatta we gonna do?"

"We could get married."

"What? Married? I wasn't planning on getting married. Not now at least. I'm tryin' to save money to buy a car… go back to college…"

"I thought you said you loved me."

"I do. But getting' married?"

Tears well up in Priscilla's eyes. "You don't love me!"

She turns away and starts to run incredibly fast down the street. Stanzo runs after her; she turns at the corner. He reaches the corner and doesn't see her anywhere. "Priscilla! Priscilla!" Stanzo shouts. He walks further down the street—looks behind cars, in front yards, and doorways. Finally, he turns and walks away in frustration.

Back at Al's, Frankie, looking rather glum and drunk sits alone. He's had a few too many drinks, and he nurses another one. He turns around to the opening door as Stanzo walks in and sits next to him. Al concentrates on the TV news. "Where is everybody? Stanzo asks.

"I don't know," Al says, "nobody's been in."

"How come you're not working tonight?" Stanzo asks, Frankie.

"I left early. My uncle's in the restaurant." He removes Gloria's engagement ring from his shirt pocket and holds it up for Stanzo to see. "Gloria broke up with me."

"'Cause of the car?"

"Yeah."

"Al, let me have a Schaefer," Stanzo says.

Al pours him the beer and watches the TV as a news reporter says, "President Johnson's landslide reelection has been overshadowed by the attack of the U.S. airbase at Bien Hoa, twelve miles north of Saigon. Under the cover of darkness, South Vietnamese forces were caught off guard by a heavy mortar attack. The Vietcong fled into the darkness without a known loss, leaving five U.S. servicemen dead and two South Vietnamese dead. Twenty-six others were wounded. In the attack, six B-52s were destroyed and twenty other aircraft were damaged. A lengthy search of the surrounding area failed to locate a single Vietcong soldier. One U.S. military official compared the attack to the Tonkin Gulf incident, implying that Americans must be prepared to accept such attacks when U.S. forces are engaged in the aid of another nation."

Al clicks off the TV and says, "This war is pissin' me off. They ain't doin' nothin' right. I went down to join the marines."

Frankie and Stanzo can't believe their ears and simultaneously say, "You?"

"Yeah. Me. Whattsa a matter with me?"

Frankie answers, "Nothin'. We're just surprised."

"Yeah, well they ain't gonna take me 'cause of my record. I would'a shown those asses how to fight this war. Ya know? I've been thinkin' about it. It's like a street fight. There's no rules in this one. The VC fight like a street gang. They hit ya when ya don't expect it. They use whatever they got for weapons. Ya got the upper hand? They leave and come back another time when you're not so strong—or don't expect it. And just like us, they can wait till the time is right for revenge." Looking at Frankie, he says, "And they don't rat on their buddies—just like us."

"I guess you're right. Well, I wish I never stole that car. I would'a been in the army and Gloria would still be my girl."

Al pours Frankie another drink. "Hey you're young. There's gonna be plenty of broads."

"I don't know, Al."

"Hey, what're ya gonna do with that ring? I might take it off your hands."

"What?" Frankie says as he and Stanzo look incredulously at Al.

"Yeah, since they won't take me into the marines, me and Anita have been talkin' about gettin' married, starting a family."

"Wow," Stanzo says.

Ricky and Nicky walk in. They sit down next to Frankie. Nicky takes papers out of his jacket pocket and puts them on the bar. "This asshole enlisted," Ricky says.

Frankie, Stanzo and Al laugh in disbelief. Nicky shows them his enlistment papers.

"Ya know my old man's been breakin' my balls. He's sure I had something to do with the stolen car. He started bitchin' at me to get a job. Now he's so proud of me. So I'll go over there and kill some gooks."

CHAPTER 23

Stanzo and Priscilla sit in her living room on a red sectional sofa with clear plastic covers. The room has nice furniture and carpet. Stanzo tries to kiss her but she pushes him away. "Stop! I don't want to," she says.

"What's a matter with you?

"Nothing."

"Where were ya last night?"

"Home."

"I called. Your mother said you were out."

"I told her to say that."

"Why?"

"I didn't feel like talking to you. And stop asking me all these questions. What are you, a detective?"

An awkward moment follows as Stanzo stares into her eyes, searching for the truth. "How do ya feel?"

"And stop asking me how I feel all the time." She shifts nervously in her seat.

"Well I'm worried about ya."

"Well don't be."

"Don't worry?"

"No." Another awkward silence follows.

Stanzo says, "I was thinkin' about us. Maybe... well... maybe we can get married."

"Maybe we can get married," Priscilla repeats sarcastically.

"Yeah, I think we can do it."

"You want to marry me because I'm pregnant or because you love me?"

"Well... both."

"Would you still want to marry me if I wasn't pregnant?"

"Yeah... I think I would. Well, but not right away."

"Then, I'm not pregnant."

Stanzo's jaw drops as he looks at her and tries to make sense out of this latest news. "You're not?"

"Yeah, I'm not."

"Why'd you tell me you were?"

"I thought I was but then I got my period. It was interesting to see what you would say."

"That's bullshit. How can you do that?"

Priscilla shrugs her shoulders indifferently. Stanzo stands up. "Ya know I believed ya when ya said ya were pregnant. Ya lied to me...how can I trust ya? And who's this sailor?"

"What sailor?"

"The one you've been seein'."

"There's no sailor."

Stanzo tries to mask his confusion and read her face. Finally, he says, "It's over between us."

"What do you mean?"

"I can't believe anything ya tell me."

"Just because you think I lied about being pregnant?"

Stanzo laughs, and says, "Yeah, ya lied about being pregnant. I don't know if you're lying about the sailor."

"So you don't want to see me anymore?"

"No."

She looks away from him. "Fine. That's the way you want it. It's fine with me too."

For a long moment, Stanzo stares at her, trying to sort things out. He says, "I just thought..." He shakes his head, gets up, and walks out of the house, leaving Priscilla staring after him.

CHAPTER 24

The day of Frankie's sentencing hearing he sits next to his attorney at the defense table. His father sits in the first row just behind them. Frankie glances over at the blonde sitting several rows back. She wears a blue sweater and short blue skirt that highlights her shapely legs. Frankie wishes he hadn't stolen her car.

On the bench, Judge Clayton reviews several documents in front of him. He looks up and addresses Frankie and his attorney. "Mister Russo, I've character references that your attorney has provided to the court, including one from the famous actor, Don Ameche. I don't know how you got that one." Frankie's about to say something, but his attorney squeezes his arm, indicating that he should be quiet. "It's unfortunate that you have committed this crime and blemished your reputation. What do you have to say for yourself?"

Frankie's attorney nudges him and Frankie stands. "Your honor, I'm very sorry about what I did." He looks over at the blonde and addresses her as much as the judge. "I don't know what I was thinking when I did it." A scowl crosses the blonde's face.

"Well Mr. Russo, I believe that you are remorseful about your crime and because you are I'm going to be lenient with you." The blonde lowers her head and shakes it in exasperation. "I've spoken to the Selective Service about you and will forward your character references and trial records to them. In my initial conversation with them, they stated that they would still consider you for military service. If you're willing to fulfill your military obligation and pay damages for the other car, this entire incident will be expunged from your record upon receiving an honorable discharge from the U.S. Army."

Frankie's head drops. The blonde doesn't look happy about the judge's sentence. The judge continues, "If you refuse to go into the military, you'll have to serve two years in the state penitentiary. I would advise you to carefully consider your options." Frankie looks over to his attorney for help.

"Your honor! Considering Mr. Russo's clean record..." Frankie's father gets the attorney's attention. "Your honor, may we take a moment to confer."

"Yes."

Frankie sits down; he, his father, and their attorney huddle together. "That's fine," Albert says. He looks at his son and he knows Frankie doesn't want to go in the army, but he also doesn't want to spend two years in jail. Frankie shrugs his shoulders hopelessly.

"Your honor. My client appreciates the court's leniency and will comply."

"Very well. I will contact the Selective Service about your decision. I'm sure they will be in touch shortly Mr. Russo. I wish you the best of luck in the army and hope you return home safely. Now see the clerk to make restitution for the stolen vehicle."

Frankie, while trying to accept the situation, doesn't notice the blonde stomping out of the courtroom.

A few days later, Charlie sits in the same place as Frankie. Judge Clayton presides once again. Charlie's mother sits behind Charlie and attorney D'Leo. The jury enters and sits. "Mister Foreman have you reached a verdict," the judge asks.

The foreman stands, facing the judge. "Yes we have your honor."

"Will the defendant please rise?" the judge says.

Charlie nervously stands. "In the case of the people versus Charles Ferraro, we find the defendant—not guilty."

A relieved smile appears on Charlie's face. His mother gasps a sigh of relief. Charlie and his attorney shake hands.

CHAPTER 25

Streamers and balloons hang from the ceiling at Al's bar. A banner over the bar reads "GOOD LUCK NICKY." A celebration for Frankie and Charlie not going to jail, and for Nicky, has been going on all night.

Slow dance '50s rock and roll plays on the jukebox. Couples in the backroom cling to each other as their bodies suggestively move to the slow grinding beat of songs like the Skyliners' "This I Swear," and "Could This Be Magic," by the Dubs.

Some of the guys sit at the bar. Everyone has consumed a lot of alcohol, even Al. Maryanne sits next to a forlorn looking Stanzo, who doesn't seem to mind being this close to her. She has her hair up and looks beautiful in a red, clingy dress. "I was sorry to hear about you and your girlfriend," she says.

Stanzo turns and looks at her for a moment. Her angelic smile seems to penetrate his apprehension towards her. "Benny, you can always talk to me. I like to listen."

"Yeah, thanks." Stanzo stares at her and seems to be seeing her as though for the first time.

Maryanne shifts uncomfortably and asks, "What's the matter?"

"You look nice."

Maryanne hesitates, then says, "Thank you." She thinks to herself, *that's the nicest thing he ever said to me*. The two sit quietly digesting their thoughts. Feeling more confident, she asks, "You wanna dance?"

Stanzo thinks a moment and says, "Sure." They get up and move to the backroom. Pinkie, sitting at the bar, watches Stanzo take Maryanne's hand in his; they put their arms around each other, bodies touching as they sway to the music. Angela, tries to dance with Nicky, but she only manages to support him as he staggers around. The ladies smile when they see Stanzo and Maryanne dancing. Anita looks over at Pinkie and gives her thumbs up.

Frankie, Ricky, and Charlie sit at the bar too drunk to notice Stanzo and Maryanne. "I could'a been goin' to jail," Frankie laments.

"What'd joor old man say?"

"He said he'd rather see me in the army than in jail."

Al walks over to them with a bottle of Seagrams 7 in his hand. He pours some in Frankie's half-empty glass and tops it off with ice and some Seven Up. "This one's on me."

"Thanks, Al."

"Ya took it on the chin and never ratted on ya friends. You're a stand-up guy."

Frankie clinks glasses with Al. "Hey, what about me?" Charlie asks.

"You're still a scumbag, but ya did the right thing—ya didn't rat on your friends either. I'm proud of you guys."

Anita, overhearing this, shakes her head and frowns. Al pours Charlie a fresh drink. Nicky has a hard time walking back to the bar. Angela supports him. With Charlie's help, the two of them hoist Nicky up on the barstool.

Nicky, slurring his words badly, says, "I'll… prob…ably be in Fort… Dix. So I'll see ya all… next… weekend."

"I'll probably be there soon, too." Frankie says as he throws more money on the bar and indicates for Al to pour himself a drink and one for Nicky, too. Al pours a shot of Johnny Walker into Nicky's glass and pours one for himself over rocks. Al raises his glass in a toast and says, "To the old days!"

They all clink glasses and repeat, "To the old days!" Nicky lifts his glass and downs it in one gulp.

Al smiles at Nicky and says, "I'm gonna miss ya. And yer probably not even gonna be around for our wedding." It surprises everyone. Anita waves her engagement ring in the air; the one Al bought from Frankie. The girls run over to Anita and congratulate her, while they admire the ring. "I'll… be back… for it," Nicky says.

"Hey, Nicky, I hear those gook girls are somethin' else. I heard about this thing they do—'around-the-world'," Charlie says.

Nicky asks, "What's… that?" Charlie elaborates. "The girl sits in a basket with a hole in it." He whispers the rest to Nicky. "They put grease on ya dick, put it through the hole and they spin the basket."

Angela overhears him, screws up her face, and looks at Charlie with disgust. "You're such a pig."

"Hey, that's no bullshit. A guy who was over there told me about it."

"No shit?" Frankie asks.

"Hey, ya... know me—I'm... game," Nicky says.

Al's attention turns to the front door as it opens and the blonde from the courthouse and her equally attractive friend walk in. She looks around, sees Frankie at the bar, and walks up to him. Frankie recognizes her immediately. She stands defiantly at his right shoulder and says, "You must think you're so smart." The guys, including Al, ogle the girls. "Stealing my car and getting away with it. I hope you find out what it feels like some day—to have your car stolen and wrecked." She stares at Frankie with scorn. Suddenly, with the quickness of a cat, she slaps him hard across the face. "There! Now I feel better."

Following the crack of that slap, a silence falls over the entire bar. They watch her and her friend turn quickly and walk out the front door, leaving them aghast. Frankie bolts off his stool and staggers his way to the door. Outside, he looks one way, and then the other. He notices the girls walking towards a white Corvette. "Hey! Hey, wait a minute!" Frankie runs towards them. They see him and quickly get into the car. Frankie catches up to them just as the engine turns over. He stands at the driver's side and says, "Hey, I'm sorry. I'm sorry about your car."

The blonde looks up at him scornfully. "My friend's goin' in the army. We're havin' a party for him. Let me buy ya a drink," Frankie says.

"A drink? I would never have a drink with you, you creep!" She steps on the gas and smoke rises up from the back wheels as she peels out of the parking space. Frankie has to jump out of the way. The car speeds down Roosevelt Avenue towards Flushing. Frankie runs after the car, and then stops. He watches and struggles to remember something as he runs back to the bar. Inside, he yells, "Al! Quick give me a pencil and paper."

Ricky laughs. "Boy, she's pissed at joo."

Frankie quickly scribbles on a napkin with the pencil. "Ya got her phone number?" Charlie asks.

Frankie looks up triumphantly. "Better, I got her license number."

"I'd watch out for that broad if I were you. She's liable to cut your balls off," Al says.

"I just have to give this number to my cop friends. I'll have her address and phone number in a couple of days."

Stanzo and Maryanne rejoin the others at the bar. Stanzo asks, "What the hell ya gonna do, steal her car again?"

"Maybe, she's got a cool Corvette." Frankie laughs. "Nah, I'm just gonna call her and apologize. Maybe, I can make it up to her."

"Oh, yeah. That's gonna happen," Stanzo says.

"We'll see."

Al says, "She's a looker alright."

"Hey, you're engaged now," Anita, reminds him.

"Hey, I can still look, can't I?"

"Did ya see her friend? She's not bad either," Charlie says.

"She has nice blond hair," Pinkie says.

"Let me know if ya get her number. I'd go out with her friend," Charlie says.

The party lasts well past Al's three a.m. closing time, and sadly, the last time they all get together.

CHAPTER 26

On a sunny, chilly afternoon, Frankie's car cruises slowly down a residential street. It stops in front of a Cape Cod style house. The car pulls up to the curb. Frankie gets out of the car with a large bouquet of assorted flowers. He walks hesitatingly to the door and rings the bell. The inside door opens. Frankie knows her name is Suzy Hamilton.

Suzy has her hair in a ponytail, and she wears a black turtleneck sweater and jeans. Frankie admires her beauty. He holds out the flowers. "Hi! These are for you." She doesn't recognize him at first, but then notices the Bonneville at the curb. Frankie smiles at her. "I wanted to apologize for stealing your car."

"You already did. So get lost! Before I call the cops."

"I wasn't sure ya heard me that night, the way ya took off."

"How'd you find out where I live?"

"How'd ya find out where I hang out?"

"I asked you first."

"Through your license plate. I got friends in the police department who can easily get that information."

"What? You're something else. You know it?"

"Yeah, I guess so. So how'd ya find me?"

"We were driving through Corona and I saw my car parked in front of that bar." She shakes her head and frowns. "Well it looked like my old car and I knew you lived in Corona."

Frankie extends the flowers. She opens the storm door hesitantly and stares at him with contempt. She takes the flowers, smells them, and looks at Frankie. Her expression quickly changes to anger. She throws the flowers in his face. "You! You! Gangster." She slams the door. Frankie hopelessly stares at the door, picks up the flowers, straightens some of them, and props them up against the door. He walks slowly to his car and drives away.

A few moments later, the door opens. Suzy comes out, picks up the flowers and looks down the street in the same direction as Frankie's car. She puts her nose to the flowers and walks back into the house with them.

The draft board delays Frankie's induction, waiting for the court to send the necessary paperwork. In the meantime, Ricky receives his draft notice and goes to basic training in Georgia. Charlie, with a promise of becoming a jet engine mechanic, joins the air force and takes basic training in Nevada. Frankie feels uneasy about leaving his father alone, but his uncle vows to pick him up and take him home after work. Frankie's young eighteen-year-old cousin, Alex, takes his place as manager at the restaurant.

Frankie thinks about Suzy all the time. When he tries calling her, he always hears the phone click on the other end. He even drives by her Bayside home a few times hoping to catch her outside. After a while, she stops answering and her mother answers the phone instead. Frankie says, "Mrs. Hamilton, I'm very sorry about stealing Suzy's car."

"Well I hope so," she says pleasantly.

Frankie explains, "It was a bad day for me. I had an accident. My fiancée turned me down when I asked her to marry me. I wasn't thinking clearly. Can you please tell that to Suzy?"

"I can't promise you anything. But I will relate to her what you just told me."

"Thank you. I'm leaving for the army soon."

"Well good luck with that. It's certainly not a good time for a young man like you to go in."

"Yes I know." Frankie gives her his phone number at home and at work and asks her to pass it on to Suzy.

At Al's Bar and Grill on New Year's Eve, Al serves a free roast beef dinner over white bread with mashed potatoes, green beans, and lots of gravy. Occasionally during the year, Al grills a hamburger for someone and charges a few bucks. That only happens a few times a year.

Frankie arrives at the bar around two-o'clock. The place has streamers hanging precariously from the ceiling, balloons bounce around on the floor, party hats, horns and noisemakers sit all around the bar. The girls wear their finest party dresses. Buck's head rests on top of the bar. Askew on his head, he wears a black cardboard top hat, only the elastic string across his forehead holds it on.

Everyone in the place looks drunk. Pinkie, Angela, and Maryanne notice Frankie first. They shout, "Happy New Year!" They run over and plant kisses on his face, leaving lipstick traces. Al waves, and extends his hand to Frankie, and shouts, "Happy New Year!"

"Yeah, Happy New Year, Al!" He shakes Al's hand. Al places a champagne glass in front of Frankie and pours from an open bottle of Andre's. "Have a glass on me."

Frankie raises his glass and shouts over the Beatle music playing on the jukebox, "Happy New Year, everyone!" Stanzo slurs, "Yeah... Happy... New Year!" Frankie and Stanzo clink glasses. Frankie looks around the bar, realizing for the first time, how much he misses Nicky, Ricky, and Charlie.

Anita comes over to Frankie, and kisses him on the cheek. "Happy New Year... Frankie," she slurs.

"Thanks, Anita. Same to you."

"Hope this is a good year for you.

"Thanks, Anita. I'm gonna need it."

"So were you busy at the restaurant tonight?" she asks.

"Yeah, the party's still going on. Lots of the Broadway people came in after their shows. My old man got tired so I took him home. I wish I was here instead. It looks like everyone had a good time."

Maryanne says, "Not really."

"We miss the guys," Angela says.

"Ya want some roast beef? I got plenty left over." Al says.

Frankie takes a sip of champagne. "Yeah, I'm starving. It was so busy tonight I didn't get a bite to eat."

"I'll go get it," Al says, and walks into the kitchen.

Hannah and Eddie from the other end of the bar raise their glasses. "Happy New Year, Frankie," they say simultaneously.

"Same to you," Frankie says as he returns the gesture.

Stanzo turns to Frankie and says, "New Year's Eve 1965. I'm… not so happy about it."

"Whattsa matter?"

"This fuckin' war stinks."

"Yeah, I know."

"When ya goin' away?"

"Any day now. I'm just waitin' to hear from them."

Al returns and places a plate of roast beef in front of Frankie. "Thanks Al!" As Frankie digs into his food, Angela, Maryanne, Pinkie, and Anita dance behind him to Elvis Presley's, "Blue Suede Shoes." Frankie turns around to watch the girls. He smiles and turns back to his food. He thinks to himself, *this place is changing, my friends are gone, and who knows what 1965 will be like.*

Frankie's last night at the restaurant and just two days before he has to leave for basic training, he gets a phone call from Suzy. "Is this Frankie?"

"Yes, it is."

"It's Suzy Hamilton."

"Oh, hi. This is a surprise." Frankie expects another lambasting, but says, "Nice of you to call me."

"So what do you want to talk to me about?"

"Hmm, I just wanted to get to know you. I have to leave for the army in two days. Can we get together for a cup of coffee or something?"

There is silence at the other end, and then finally, she says, "I don't think so."

"Oh, come on, it's just a cup of coffee.

"Well I got school tomorrow."

"Where do you go to school."

"Hofstra University."

"What time do ya get out?"

"Around two-thirty."

"Why don't we meet then?"

Surprisingly, Suzy agrees and the day before his induction, they meet in a Flushing coffee shop. She looks beautiful in tight fitting jeans, and a brown turtleneck sweater that highlights her blond hair. She even smiles at him when she sits down at the booth. "You look very pretty," Frankie says.

She attempts a smile and seems friendlier than previously. "Thank you." They order coffees and both relax a little. "So you're leaving tomorrow."

"Yeah, I'm going to Fort Dix."

She sips at her coffee. "That's not too far from home."

"Yeah, I should be able to get back here a few times."

"How does your family feel about it?"

"It's just my father. My mother died of cancer when I was fourteen. You probably saw him sitting behind me in court. He's not happy about it, but he'd rather see me in the army than in jail."

Suzy looks at him with disdain. "I wanted you to go to jail. To teach you a lesson."

"Yeah, I know."

"I'll feel bad if you have to go to Vietnam, though. I don't like wars."

"Thanks."

"So your fiancée broke up with you?"

Looking down and not feeling like talking about it, Frankie says, "Yeah. How about you? You have a boyfriend?"

She hesitates to answer and pushes some hair away from her rosy cheek. "Well the same thing happened to me. My fiancée broke up with me." She stares him straight in the eye and raises her voice. "The same week that you stole my car!"

Frankie feels even worse now. He tries to shift the conversation and says, "You see we have a lot in common. And we even like the same cars."

Suzy relaxes a little more and forces a smile.

"What's your major?"

"History with a minor in education. I'm in my junior year. I want to teach high school history."

The meeting lasts more than an hour and the two depart, agreeing to write to each other.

CHAPTER 27

Several months later, Frankie completes basic and advanced infantry training. He returns home on leave with orders for Vietnam. He tells everyone that he ran into JoJo at Fort Dix, and he had a beer with him. During the whole time, Frankie and Suzy keep in touch. She even visits him at Fort Dix one weekend.

At Al's, Suzy sits next to Frankie. Things in Corona keep changing as more and more neighborhood guys go into the service. Al and his older clientele don't like the hippie revolution with its drugs and unusual way of dressing.

Stanzo sits at the bar next to Maryanne. He sports a big Fu Man Chu mustache, and long flowing hair, a stark contrast to Frankie's military haircut. Stanzo wears a bright orange and paisley shirt, wide bellbottom jeans, and Fry boots.

Pinkie has cut Maryanne's hair in an Afro style. With her new hairdo, Maryanne wears a low-cut white blouse, beads around her neck, a brown leather vest, and bell-bottom jeans. Pinkie and Angela replace their tough-girl street look of black leather for bright colors, long flowing dresses, and paisley headbands. Pinkie sports dark granny glasses.

Suzy wears a tie-dye t-shirt of orange, blue, yellow, and green. On her head she wears a black, priest-like fedora, bell-bottoms, and a peace symbol hangs around her neck. She and Frankie have marriage plans when he gets out of the army, but he hasn't given her an engagement ring yet.

Al's not happy about this "hippie thing," as he calls it, because nobody drinks anymore; they all smoke pot.

"Al, give me an orange juice this time," Stanzo says.

"Hey Stanzo, orange juice is for screwdrivers. Ya want orange juice, go have breakfast."

"Come on Al... So charge me for a screwdriver without the vodka."

Reluctantly, Al fills a glass with orange juice and takes enough money to cover a screwdriver. "How come they never draft you?"

"He's only got one kidney," Maryanne answers.

"Oh, yeah. I forgot," Al says.

Something on TV catches Al's attention. He turns up the volume. The newscaster says, "Secretary of State Robert McNamara has referred to the Vietnam War as a 'dirty little war.' Casualty figures have reached 425 killed and another 2,200 wounded."

"I'm not surprised." Al turns to his customers sitting at the bar and says, "Ya know, they're lying to us. They inflate these body counts to make it look like we're winnin'."

"Ya think so?" Frankie asks.

"Yeah, I'm sure that's what they're doin'. They're kickin' our asses every day."

"Hey Al, we're kickin' their asses, too," Frankie says.

"That's what they're tellin' you army guys. Ya think wounded and body bags is kickin' ass? I got news for ya..."

Just then, the news shows an anti-war protest going on. Al says, "It's these goddamn protesters. Ya think they're helpin' any? Goddamn Communists."

"Yeah, well I'm worried about Nicky," Angela says.

Frankie says, "I got a letter from him today. I got it with me." He removes the letter from his jacket pocket.

"Let's hear it. Isn't he on helicopters?" Al asks.

"Yeah," Frankie says.

"Ya know he's in the shit." Al says.

"He's always in the shit," Stanzo adds and laughs.

Angela says anxiously, "Read it to us." They all gather around Frankie.

"Dear Frankie. I can't believe you're coming over here. I hope we see each other. I sure miss hangin' around Al's—bullshittin' and getting' drunk. Heard from Ricky the other day. He's probably comin' over here, too. We should all plan to meet in Saigon some time and party. I've only been there once so far but I had a ball. It's nothing like Corona. I'll take you guys to some cool places to get high and laid. They got some dynamite weed over here."

Al interrupts saying, "That asshole's fuckin' around with that shit, too!" He stares at Stanzo with contempt.

"Hey, cool it! Let me finish... 'We've been pickin' up guys wounded near the Cambodian Border. It gets pretty hairy sometimes. Charlie shoots at you from the trees. But our guys fry their asses with napalm. Some of the guys we pick up never make it to the hospital."

"That's a bitch," Stanzo says.

"I heard Charlie joined the air force. Those flyboys don't see the kind of shit we do, but it's sure nice to have them around sometimes. Hey, but you know me. I'm always up for a good fight, but I'd rather be back there hangin' out at Al's. How is that old fuck anyway?" Al shakes his fist at an imaginary Nicky. "Tell him I probably won't be back in time for his wedding. I feel sorry for Anita. She could'a had me instead." Hearing this Anita laughs; there are a few giggles around the bar. "Say hi to Stanzo for me. That one-kidney'd son-of-a-bitch. And tell the girls I miss them."

Angela with tears running down her cheeks says, "We love ya, Nicky!"

Maryanne and Pinkie add their sentiments.

Frankie continues reading. "I'm lookin' forward to bein' back in the states in eight months. I'm gonna try to get an early out. It's nice to get letters at mail call, so tell everybody to write. My address is on the envelope." Frankie holds it up for everyone to see. "My old man writes me every day. He says that's what kept him goin' in the big one. I don't know if you've seen him lately, but the old lady says I'm all he talks about. The asshole's so proud that I'm in the war. Have a drink for me. Your Friend, Nicky."

Frankie holds up a sheet of paper with a caricature of Nicky hanging from the skid of a helicopter with tracer bullets flying all around him. Everyone starts talking loudly as Al fiddles with the TV antenna, trying to improve the reception. President Johnson's image appears on the screen. Al tells them, "Shut up! Let's hear what the president had to say."

A newscaster says, "President Johnson in his press conference tonight referred to our young men as 'the flower of our youth.' He regrets with great sorrow having to send them into battle, but reiterated that we cannot dishonor our word or our commitment to the people of South Vietnam as long as there are men who hate and destroy. He went on to say that this is why we are in Vietnam."

EPILOGUE

Corona was never the same after that—everything changed. Nobody drank anymore. Everyone smoked pot. Al and Anita got married, he sold the bar, and they moved to Tampa, Florida.

Charlie was on an air force transport that went down in a fiery crash in the Vietnam Highlands. There wasn't even a body to send home to his mother. Nicky was never the same when he came back. He was nervous, jumpy and moody, and then he got into some heavy drugs. Ricky never came back; he was missing in action. Stanzo finally got enough money together to buy a car and go back to Queens College, and eventually law school. He became a civil rights attorney in Washington, D.C. He and Maryanne dated for a while but eventually broke up.

Pinkie went to work in her uncle's funeral home. Angela tried to have a relationship with Nicky when he came home, but drugs took over his life, and she tired of competing with his addiction. Maryanne finished college and became a kindergarten teacher. It turned out Priscilla wasn't married to anyone and she never came around anymore. Pinkie was the only one who saw her after Priscilla and Stanzo broke up.

Little by little, most everyone moved out of Corona and lost touch with one another. Eddie and Hannah continued to live upstairs and frequented the bar as usual under the new owner. They found Buck dead in his apartment one day. No one knew about his diabetes—that and alcohol caused him to have a stroke.

Wounded in Vietnam, they sent Frankie home with shrapnel in his back before the end of his tour of duty. His father suffered a heart attack when he received the news. While Frankie recuperated in a New York VA hospital, he received an invitation to Gloria's wedding—the only time she ever wrote to him. He declined the invitation, sent a gift and best wishes.

Frankie received a purple heart and the court cleared his record as they had promised. Not long after that Frankie's father had a fatal heart attack and died. Eventually, Frankie and his uncle sold the restaurant. After a few years, the wounds Frankie received in Vietnam put him in a wheelchair.

The strangest and best thing that came of the whole story—Frankie and Suzy got married. She taught high school history until they started a family. Frankie and Suzy had two boys and a girl.

Frankie bought a used car lot in Long Island not far from his home in Kings Park. He would scoot around the lot in his electric wheelchair selling cars. Frankie bought Suzy a new car every year of their marriage. Oddly enough, Suzy would never let Frankie drive her car. Frankie accepted this as her way of punishing him for stealing her Bonneville in 1964.

ACKNOWLEDGMENTS

"Midnight Auto Supply" is an adaption of my award-winning screenplay "Big White Bonneville." In the year 2000, the Colorado Council on the Arts awarded me a fellowship for that screenplay. I subsequently produced it as a short film entitled, "My Bonneville" that became popular at film festivals around the country.

In this adaptation, I started out writing a novel based on the original screenplay. To my best efforts, the story is concise, well written with well drawn-out characters, but short. Much to my initial surprise, it has become a novella.

I am forever thankful to my wife, Anita, for her love and support. She's always patient and I rely on her intuition, good taste and help in editing my work.

In addition to Anita, I have to thank my good friend Harvey Castro for his continued support and for reading my early drafts; I value his feedback and opinions. Attorney Bill Carter, my neighbor and friend, also read the book and provided helpful information about some of the legal aspect of the story.

My writer friend, Betty Barkman, read the book and offered her opinions in which I am especially grateful.

My editor and cover designer, Kym O'Connell-Todd, has helped me to polish this work and her cover design has hit the mark once again.

I'm also grateful to Sandy Cortner, Craig Dirgo, George Sibley and Larry Meredith, all fine writers in their own right, for reading the book and offering helpful opinions.

Thanks also to my dear friend, Tootsie Schreiber, who provided additional editing help.

I would like to thank my friend, Robert F. Lyons, Director, who helped me to visualize "My Bonneville" and to bring it to the screen. There were so many people to thank in that production. To name a few, Lew Dauber, David O'Donnell, Tori McPetrie, Michael Wiseman, Jason Pace, David De Angelis, Ivan Basso, and Anthony Dietel, whose acting brought my characters to life. Behind the screen, many thanks go to Rozanne Taucher, David Plane, Richard Strauss, Michael Frenchman, Karen Crowe, Greg Cannella, Kevin A. West and Paulo Andres of the Actors' Network, and our friends at Echo Entertainment in Los Angeles.

I would not be an author today without thanking my old friend Carolyn Margon, who many years ago encouraged me to write and this was the first story I tried writing. Lastly, I must say thank you to the late Syd Fields, who taught me how to write screenplays, and the skills he taught me I still use today in my writing.

ABOUT THE AUTHOR

"Midnight Auto Supply" is Bob Puglisi's second novel. His first one "Railway Avenue" continues to grow in popularity. His non-fiction memoir "Almost A Wiseguy," tells the story about his friend, Vince Ciacci's, life in the Mafia, and his struggles with alcohol and drug addiction. Vince's story is also the subject matter of a series of podcasts at *www.mobshotpodcast.com*.

Bob has had a varied background from IT professional, actor, playwright, producer, and librarian at the Old Rock Library in Crested Butte, Colorado. His stage plays have been produced in Los Angeles and at the Crested Butte Mountain Theatre in his hometown. His acting credits include stage, film and television. Some of his memorable TV roles were on "Matlock" with the late Andy Griffith, "Hill Street Blues," and several appearances in comedy skits on "The Tonight Show with Jay Leno."